Opium and Other Stories

by GÉZA CSÁTH

Selected and with a Biographical Note
by Marianna D. Birnbaum

Translated by Jascha Kessler
and Charlotte Rogers

Introduction by Angela Carter

PENGUIN BOOKS

Penguin Books Ltd, Harmondsworth,
Middlesex, England
Penguin Books, 40 West 23rd Street,
New York, New York 10010, U.S.A.
Penguin Books Australia Ltd, Ringwood,
Victoria, Australia
Penguin Books Canada Limited, 2801 John Street,
Markham, Ontario, Canada L3R 1B4
Penguin Books (N.Z.) Ltd, 182–190 Wairau Road,
Auckland 10, New Zealand

First published in the United States of America
under the title *The Magician's Garden and Other Stories*
by Columbia University Press 1980
Published in Penguin Books 1983

LIBRARY OF CONGRESS CATALOGING IN PUBLICATION DATA
Csáth, Géza, 1887–1919.
   Opium and other stories.
   (Writers from the other Europe)
   Reprint. Originally published: The magician's
garden and other stories. New York: Columbia
University Press, 1980.
   I. Birnbaum, Marianna D. II. Title. III. Series.
PH3213.C69A24   1983   894'.51133   83-2170
ISBN 0 14 00.6689 6

Printed in the United States of America by
R.R. Donnelley & Sons Company, Harrisonburg, Virginia

The illustrations are from Attila Sassy's volume *Ópium-álmok*
(*Opium Dreams*), published in 1909.

WRITERS FROM THE OTHER EUROPE

The purpose of this paperback series is to bring together outstanding and influential works of fiction by Eastern European writers. In many instances they will be writers who, though recognized as powerful forces in their own cultures, are virtually unknown in the West. It is hoped that by reprinting selected Eastern European writers in this format and with introductions that place each work in its literary and historical context, the literature that has evolved in "the other Europe," particularly during the postwar decades, will be made more accessible to a new readership.

PHILIP ROTH

OTHER TITLES IN THIS SERIES

*Ashes and Diamonds**
by Jerzy Andrzejewski
Introduction by Heinrich Böll

*The Book of Laughter and
Forgetting*
by Milan Kundera
Afterword: A Talk with the
Author by Philip Roth

Closely Watched Trains
by Bohumil Hrabal
Introduction by Josef Škvorecký

The Farewell Party
by Milan Kundera
Introduction by Elizabeth Pochoda

Laughable Loves
by Milan Kundera
Introduction by Philip Roth

*Sanatorium under the Sign
of the Hourglass*
by Bruno Schulz
Introduction by John Updike

The Street of Crocodiles
by Bruno Schulz
Introduction by Jerzy Ficowski

*This Way for the Gas,
Ladies and Gentlemen**
by Tadeusz Borowski
Introduction by Jan Kott

*A Tomb for Boris Davidovich**
by Danilo Kiš
Introduction by Joseph Brodsky

*Available in Great Britain

Table of Contents

Introduction

The circumstances of Géza Csáth's brief, unhappy life are those of a child of the death throes of an empire, of a time when the public fictions that hitherto held disparate groups of people together are no longer capable of sustaining belief. At these times, a marked tendency reveals itself for the individual to look inward for sources of, shall we say, truth, because the fragmented society, like shards of a broken mirror, reflects too many possible truths. Csáth's fiction is grounded in such a sense of individual isolation, and he found the tensions inside himself, finally, too great to be borne.

The Austro-Hungarian Empire, in which Csáth was born, was a kind of dream, as all empires are, sustained by the vast bureaucracy, paranoid as a dream, that so haunted Kafka. Many of the constituent parts of that empire are now client states of another kind of imperialism; Eastern Europe is now, in its economic and political organization, as alien to the West as the other side of the moon. But the territory eventually administered by the old empire, with its complex social and ethnic groupings, its babel of tongues, its constantly shifting borders, its states that sometimes disappeared altogether, bore, in the nineteenth and early twentieth century, the same relation to the Western European imagination as Latin America does to that of the United States today. It was the location of the vague Ruritania of Edwardian romance, of innumerable operettas, perceived from the outside as exotic, and, from the inside, certainly in the fiction of

Csáth, as a loveless and sinister community of small-minded individuals engaged, sometimes literally, in rending one another to pieces.

Inhabitant of a collective dream, Csáth, the opium addict and therefore a specialist in dreams, wrote short stories comfortless as bad dreams, sometimes decorating them languorously with art-nouveau impedimenta of lilies, lotuses, and sulphurous magic, at other times relating them in the cool, neutral language of the case-book. He was also a doctor. No real contradiction here; the medical profession not only offers free access to narcotics but often, since it involves considerable exposure to human suffering, implicitly invites their use.

Csáth's short stories are an extraordinary, uneasy mixture of sentimentality, sadism, and sexual repression — nasty tales, not dissimilar to some of the fictions of the contemporary United States and United Kingdom, both countries in which the collective dream has, latterly, also broken down under the impact of too much reality. During Csáth's lifetime Sigmund Freud, the scrutineer of dreams, built up the enormous hypothesis of the unconscious in Vienna, the greatest city of the empire — which encompassed Hungary, Csáth's homeland, more and more uneasily. It is difficult to read Csáth, a specialist in "nervous disorders" himself, without thinking of Freud's analyses of the subtexts of human experience, because Csáth was tortured by the ambiguities of that experience.

Some of Csáth's stories center on drugs and suggest he could think of no way out of the treacherous minefield of human experience; that, most of all, he wanted an end of it — but, although death is the only foolproof way of evading reality, he, a young man, full of talent, didn't want to die, yet, not quite yet. . . . So he searched, with the diligence of the obsessive, for a life drained of the necessary discomforts of actual living. Drugs! the obvious answer; " . . . the tiny opium pipe will lead you to where we live for the sake of Life alone and nothing more." It's a funny kind of life, viewed from the operating end of an opium pipe or a morphine syringe; life seen as a kind of existential freedom, not to act — but to do nothing. "I shoot up, therefore I exist." To exist, perhaps, but not to be. In "Opium," Csáth posits life as a kind of pure distillate of inactivity, locked in the stasis induced by the drug. The drug that does not so much heal pain as freeze it, or, rather, freeze you, so you can't feel pain anymore.

The alcoholic surgeon in "The Surgeon" prescribes absinthe as a solvent for time; but, opium . . . ah! Opium gives the illusion of an infinitely extended duration, does not so much dissolve time as slow it down to a Jurassic pace. "Hence in one single day I live a thousand years. . . . "

And if this sense of profoundly extensible time creates the vertigo of Andrew Marvell's "deserts of vast eternity," Csáth is sufficiently seduced by the fin-de-siècle glamour of narcotics addiction to decorate those deserts with evil flowers, perfumed and lugubrious, such as blossom in "The Magician's Garden" — even though these flowers are, alas, already somewhat dog-eared, since they have been arranged and rearranged by a century of self-conscious decadents from Thomas De Quincey to Charles Baudelaire. It must have been this awareness of his impeccable credentials among that company of damned souls, the nineteenth-century underground with its accessories of pipe, tincture bottle, and syringe, that accounts for one of the oddest characteristics of the unnerving fiction of Csáth: its complacency. Nobody so smug as the junky, who knows quite well how daring it is to glut on the forbidden.

There is a similar sense of complacency at his own daring in the subclinical expositions of that "real life" he must often have visited as a stranger. Some of the finest of these stories — for Csáth's slight self-satisfaction at his own unshockableness does not prevent these stories from being very fine — depend upon the reader's presumption of the innocence of children so that Csáth can overthrow that presumption. For he likes to write about children who, on a whim, will maim and murder.

These are the truly polymorphously perverse brats of the Freudian scenario, small beings without conscience or guilt who will stop at nothing for their own gratification, products of family relationships in a state of terminal pathology, evidence in themselves of the decay of the bourgeois-liberal underpinnings of the last years of the unwieldy Hapsburg dinosaur — though this is a point Csáth makes but leaves unstressed.

Yet, cumulatively, the activities of these children of our worst fears produce an unintentionally comic effect. As Csáth's little horrors get on with their games of cutting up cats, firing houses, lynching dachshunds, and worse, the spirit of Edward Gorey seems to hover over the narratives. God help their babysitters, one thinks. But black humor is not quite Csáth's style. He perceives with atrocious clarity the monomaniacal self-centeredness of the child, any ordinary child, who, deprived of candy, cries "I'll kill you!" and means it, though he doesn't know quite what he means, only that he'd prefer the barrier to his gratification should cease to exist. After all, most of us behaved like that, once. But most of us, willy-nilly, acquire conscience and guilt through the mediation of other people. So we learn how to be human beings. But Csáth, who perceives human society as a Hobbesian nightmare of self-centeredness, must have thought that conscience was innate (although nobody who has spent much time with small children can think that for long). That conscience was innate; and the lack of it in children is a sign of — what? Evil? The inherent depravity of the human condition?

But his "little horrors," most of them just about prepubescent, appall because they continue to behave, in later childhood, with the egotistical logic of the infant — when they have the physical means to carry out their desires. They are like those children who have been stowed away in cupboards or outhouses as babies, "feral children" who have been denied access to the processes of socialization and who, therefore, become exiles from humanity. Without conscience, without guilt, they do dreadful things and there is no hope for them, none at all, and hence no hope for the world they might grow up to make. For Csáth, evidently, has no *faith* in children, and, therefore, in the future.

Since Csáth always scrupulously refrains from referring to notions of morality, there is a kind of corrupt sentimentality about his refusal to pass judgment, about the way he describes these crimes of childhood as if they *came naturally* to those who commit them. It is as though he shrugs and says: "That's how it is." Yet these stories somehow seem to mean more than they say, and this is the point at which Csáth becomes a significant writer — in those stories of his where the flesh of a cruel narrative may be seen to conceal the phosphorescent bones of certain real terrors. Where he hints at the unspeakable — certain themes for which there was no real language available to him — by means of the unmentionable — the things we don't like to talk about in polite society. Where he hints at, for example, incestuous desire for the mother, the "unspeakable" taboo, by means of a description of the murder of the mother, which, though it may be a most humanly terrible crime, does indeed happen. And "Matricide" might have taken its plot from any newspaper, "unmentionable" in a drawing room but not in a court of law or a forensic laboratory.

"Matricide" is about two little boys, fatherless children, who entertain themselves by torturing small animals while their indifferent mother reads cheap novels and keeps company with a clerk. The first line of the story is viciously ironic: "When fathers of fine, healthy children die, there's trouble." This is the voice of the plain common sense of unimaginative people expressing itself in a language almost ludicrously inadequate to the kind of "trouble" the Witman boys get themselves into. Besides, the lack of a father is not the real problem; the boys seem to have been born psychopathic sadists. "Their curiosity over the mystery of pain was insatiable." (As it might be, might it not, for a medical man at a time when anesthesia was still in its infancy? Such curiosity need not be pathological.)

But neglect offers the Witman boys ample opportunity to indulge that curiosity: "Animal torture grew into a serious, ordinary passion with them." They catch, mutilate, and finally kill an owl; that very day, the older boy strays into a brothel and embraces a girl. "Witman's elder son thought of the owl: through his mind it flashed — why is everything in life that is beautiful, exciting and wonderful so inexplicably horrible and bloody, too." He takes his brother to the girl. Making love to the whore is even more fun than torturing the owl.

The boys become "full of hatred for their blonde, blue-eyed mother. They'd have liked to torture her, too." They murder her in the course of robbing her to pay for further pleasures. In effect, they kill their mother to pay the whore, as though matricide were the price of sexual experience.

But it isn't as simple as that; the boys kill their mother in explicitly erotic circumstances: "the elder Witman boy leaped towards her bed and plunged his knife into her breast." After she is dead, the boy says: "Well, everything's under control." But just *what* is under control? Could it be the sexual threat, to which they have just been awakened, which this dead woman can no longer pose?

Cool as a court reporter, Csáth has related these events as they might be disclosed in a court of law: the boys' gruesome hobbies, the whore, the robbery, the murder. And, however disquieting, the story can stand as a metaphor for the way in which becoming an adult oneself involves the destruction of the idea of the parent. But the erotic circumstances of the death of this mother suggest a deeper transgression for which there is no metaphor, the "unspeakable" incestuous threat Mrs. Witman poses while she lives.

Csáth stresses Mrs. Witman is still young, still pretty, and still, however indolently, sexually active. Further, the boys are given no names of their own but are always referred to by their relation to the dead father — the Witman boys, Witman's elder son, his younger son — and in this way they are distanced in the narrative from their own mother, with whom there is no real affection. And, because Csáth, under the surface of the story, is dealing with universal ambiguities of relationships, it is something of a consolation to know that the Witman boys are not, after all, supposed to be "normal"; they are psychopathic, lack a father's guidance, suffer an indifferent mother.

But even if Mrs. Witman *is* an indifferent, an unmotherly mother, that does not explain why her sons don't love her. Perhaps they don't love her just because she is still young and pretty and plump, provoking not filial devotion but desire. Perhaps they don't love her just because, until they put a stop to it, she is alive.

Woman-as-mother, in Csáth, is most loved when dead, not a threat but a memory. There is less thematic difference between his dreamy, secessionist fairy tales and his "realist" narratives than might appear. The haunting "Meeting Mother," which begins "My mother died giving me birth," concerns a lovely young ghost encountered in a dream after the narrator has "come back late from a woman" (presumably a prostitute). The apparition of this beloved stranger, just as she was when she died at twenty years of age, is accompanied by exquisitely symbolist music, a harp, a flute — you can almost hear them, scored by Debussy or

Fauré. In his dream, the narrator covers her "girl's breasts — that had never suckled me" with lilies of the valley. The time comes to part. "I wanted to hug my lovely mother yet one last time. She looked at me with an offended expression, but then stroked my face forgivingly."

Since this dream, the narrator has abandoned all earthly women and thinks only of his mother, who "died sighing long and hard." Died sighing a sigh as of erotic satisfaction, in fact, although in the dream she has both acknowledged the existence of an incest taboo by forbidding that last embrace yet also forgiving the narrator for wanting it.

This dream consolation of the mother/not mother, who bore the narrator but did not suckle him, who is fixed as a young girl in the amber of death, adds to the already heavy burden of forbidden incestuous desire the further spiritual and psychological hazard of necrophilia. It is no wonder, given all this, that the narrator now turns away from earthly women, who represent, apart from anything else, betrayal.

Interestingly enough, Csáth's own mother died, not in his early infancy, but when he was nine years old, old enough to have acquired a cargo of authentic and hence necessarily ambivalent memory. About the age, perhaps, of the younger Witman boy.

Another dreamy story, actually titled "An Afternoon Dream," contains a variation on the idea of the mother/not mother, a woman who can only love after she has wept over the coffin of her dead child. (In a time of high infant mortality, this idea must have seemed less deliberately perverse than it does today.) This rambling story, with its truly dreamlike incoherence and paraphernalia of magic and wizards reminiscent of the late-nineteenth-century vogue for literary fairy tales (Hans Andersen, of whom Csáth was fond; Oscar Wilde; Hugo von Hofmannsthal) weaves around this central paradox of the mother/not mother, as if in some way attempting to negate the reproductive capacity of the woman, since only this negation will permit sexual and emotional access to her.

In another dreamy story, "Joseph in Egypt," the dreamer encounters a woman who, unusual in Csáth, fully expresses what William Blake called "the lineaments of gratified desire." She is statuesque, opulent. "The gorgeous blue rings beneath her eyes suggested rich years of womanly knowledge and life's pleasures." She, too, is a mother/not mother, since she is married but as yet without children: "A holy man from Asia prophesied that I shall have them and so I wait in patience." Neither dead herself nor the mother of dead children, but, rather, a mother *in potentia*, she may be desired without restraint, but also — without consummation. "You must leave now — do you want me to die?" she asks. She is married. The punishment for adultery is death. The dreamer leaves her. When he wakes, she haunts him.

"I envied Joseph his having had such a beautiful dream," concludes Csáth baldly. And he does not claim *this* dream as his own but ascribes it to the legendary dreamer of the Old Testament, to Joseph, who dreamed prophecies. But *this* dream invokes the third party in the oedipal triangle often most present, in Csáth's fiction, by his absence — the rival, the man to whom intercourse with the mother *is* permitted, that is, her husband, that is, your father. That father, who in the little genre story "Saturday Evening," a cozy glimpse of a family supper table, does appear as paterfamilias and, in this role, takes mother off to bed, while the ominous Sandman, the bogeyman, watches over everything.

There is the truly strange "Father, Son," told in terms of absolute realism and most strange, perhaps, because it could have sprung from a real event; it has just the quality of those macabre anecdotes beloved of medical students (as have one or two other stories, in particular "Trepov on the Dissecting Table"). A young man arrives at the Institute of Anatomy, looking for his father's corpse, which has been deposited there for medical research. He plans to rescue the corpse and bury it. It turns out that the Institute of Anatomy has already boiled down the corpse and reassembled it as a skeleton, for the instruction of the medical students. The son of the skeleton takes it away in his arms. "He was hurrying his strange burden off, determinedly. But averting his eyes, as if blushing for his father."

The father is, quite literally, the "skeleton in the closet" of the English idiom. The little story recalls, in a mode of grotesque irony, how Virgil's Aeneas carries his aged father on his back from the ruins of Troy. But, for Csáth, the past is not a living entity but a bundle of dry bones. To take them away for burial is an act without meaning. Indeed, it deprives the poor skeleton of any posthumous usefulness in the world — after all, the skeleton *was* performing a useful function in the Institute of Anatomy, an instructive function, which is one of the real functions of parenthood.

"Father, Son" is a tiny but perfect image of a relation to the past, to the individual's own history, that has lost any personal significance. Indeed, the father might also stand for the emperor, the father of his people, whose authority was already, in Csáth's Hungary, seen as empty form and whose rule would collapse amid a welter of corpses with the conclusion of the First World War, in which Csáth fought.

Another story, "Railroad," describes the humiliation of a paterfamilias with almost gloating satisfaction, a humiliation that has all the more disastrous effect upon the poor man because, out of shame, he decides to keep it to himself. If this is a small tragedy about the deleterious effects of bourgeois manners, nevertheless here the father is incompetent, inadequate, unable to cope with the simplest operations of the reality principle.

The father in Csáth, therefore, is more of an embarrassment than a rival or a threat. In "Paul and Virginia," a cool exercise in irony, a woman claims the legal father of her daughter is not the natural father, thus permitting the girl to marry.

This is an odd story, partly because its initial premise seems, in the late twentieth century, utterly arcane; how, simply, odd that first cousins need apply to a "higher authority" for permission to marry. How odd, too, that the sophisticated and "unshockable" Csáth should present the mother's admission of adultery as a heroic form of social hara-kiri rather than as the cynical maneuver that would undoubtedly have been presented by Csáth's Viennese contemporary, Arthur Schnitzler. And, in this story, both fathers, the legal and the natural, disappear; neither has a speaking or acting role. They are matters of form. The content is all between mother and daughter, and the cruelty of the virtuous Virginia, whose very name evokes that archetypal romance of primal innocence, Bernardin de Saint-Pierre's "Paul et Virginie." This Virginia, however, "would have let her mother go to torture had her own happiness depended on it." (The image of the child torturing its mother, again.)

Other European contemporaries of Csáth besides Schnitzler — Ibsen, say, or Wedekind — might have used the same plot to point up the social hypocrisy that surrounds the young lovers, that wishes to deny their perfectly legitimate desire to consummate the love they have felt for each other since childhood. Csáth, however, is seduced by the notion of the suffering this pure love produces. He prefers to leave the story as a simple description of the cruel selfishness of the individual, in particular, the girl, Virginia — Paul himself doesn't have much say in the matter — as she pursues her personal gratification. He even applauds his own refusal to castigate Virginia: "there's no reason *I* should be angry at her for it." But since there is indeed no reason at all, it is strange he should make a virtue out of pretending not to judge her. Because he *is* implicitly judging her; the girl's willingness to grasp happiness without regard for her mother is treated as the bitterest irony. He does not treat with irony the arbitrary rules of this society that forces young lovers and their allies to such stratagems. Csáth, it turns out, is not one to question the bases of the society that produces these cruelties. He prefers to see cruelty as one of the inevitable facts of life. Perhaps that is why he was so unhappy.

The scarcely characterized Paul is no more than the thing that will make Virginia happy by, presumably, removing the virginity for which she is named, since to marry, for a bourgeois Hungarian virgin of this period, is the only way to make love. It is apparent that Csáth does not regard his heroine's desire to do *that* as in the least legitimate. If this story veils discreetly the fear of female sexuality unmediated by motherhood (although, like the Witman boys, Virginia destroys her mother in pursuit of sexual gratification), another story, "The Pass," expresses it with startling vividness.

In "The Pass" the lewd, unmotherly, nude bodies of women form the actual landscape of the narrative, a landscape that is inherently inimical. "The Pass" is written in the style of Csáth's dream visions, but, since he does not tell us that it *is* a dream, the story may be categorized in the problematic area of the "fantastic," in which the metaphor itself is the meaning.

A young man starts off on a journey and encounters first one giant, heroic, languid female nude, then another, and then another until: "they filled all the roads and the horizon, too. Awesome, a horrible and mute blockade." Finally the boy falls, "sinking into the seductive, magnetic force." The women have overwhelmed him. The (male) narrator waits for a long time, "rigid with grief," but the boy never reappears.

It is as curious an experience for a woman to read this story as it is for an African to read Conrad's "Heart of Darkness." Csáth uses the form of the fantastic as a device to extract all the reality from the idea of Woman; these women are nothing but huge objects, alien and menacing to just the degree they are beautiful and desirable. And, if objects, they are highly motivated objects. They want that boy . . . and they get him. He disappears among them as in a swamp. I'm tempted, of course, to make cheap jokes: "Can one man be so attractive to women?" And: "He should be so lucky." Since, in this way, I can evade the real hostility in Csáth's image of a fully sexualized landscape that destroys life to just the degree that this landscape is female, as if the female was somehow not natural or as if, in Baudelaire's phrase, it is abominable just because it is natural. This sexualized terrain threatens the fragile autonomy of the boy with an erotic power that must destroy him.

Best, perhaps, to murder the girl-child while she is still pubescent, as in "Little Emma." A group of children play at public executions with predictably disastrous consequences for "the prettiest of my kid sister Irma's friends." The child narrator himself puts the noose round Emma's neck and helps her onto the improvised scaffold: "It was the first chance I'd ever had to hold Emma in my arms."

But this story, perhaps the finest in this collection, allows the outside world to obtrude upon the children and to help shape them. Unlike the Witman boys, they are not born sadists; they are real children in which the ethical neutrality of children has been precociously warped by the institutionalized violence around them, the "normal" violence of society. In the first part of the story, the narrator describes how he has been made distraught by a savage beating inflicted on a schoolfellow by a teacher. They are a military family, the father a major. The narrator's brother, who invents the game of cutting up the cat with a carving knife, will grow up to be an army officer — although the narrator himself, we are told, will eventually kill himself. The children invent the game of hanging after reading a graphic account of a public execution in the newspapers, an account which has provoked their father to describe an execution he once saw himself. It is in this context that the narrator, who truly adores his little Emma, can help to hang her, as if hanging will not kill her, not hurt her.

Or — as if death will preserve her *as* a beloved child, eternally in white stockings with the pink ribbon in her braids. For a corpse poses no threats. Even if, since the boy is doomed to suicide, such a corpse might exert a posthumous revenge.

The tensions within Csáth, which produced these strange tales that question so much yet leave so much unquestioned, take perhaps the most disturbing form in a story of murderous children that concerns itself not with virgin girls or mothers, but with brothers, and cracks open on that gulf of darkness which is beyond questioning.

In "The Black Silence" the little brother grows up "between one day and another," turns overnight from a "lovely little toddler" into a ravening monster who roasts a kitten over a slow flame, robs, commits arson. Taken to a madhouse, the boy escapes, runs home. His father is powerless to deal with him; his elder brother strangles him while he sleeps. Then a transformation takes place: "A little weak child lay in the bed," changed back in death into the darling toddler he used to be.

Or, perhaps . . . always was. For this tale is told to a doctor: "Doctor, I'm writing down what this is all about" — and its teller need not necessarily be trusted. All we know for certain, all he has *really* told us, is — that he has murdered his brother. Who is the monster, here?

And with the last words of the story, in their shocking and deliberate bathos — "As a matter of fact, Doctor, I can never get a good night's sleep" — we understand we have not been reading a story about bad children, or even about sibling rivalry, a theme which makes no other appearance in Csáth, but about insanity. About that place where life is indeed lived "for the sake of Life alone," in the frozen isolation of madness. About that black silence which Csáth, the specialist in nervous disorders, must have studied with a clinical objectivity that was a defense against his own fears, the insanity that was his own melancholic fate among the final ruins of the social order in which he had all his short life found so little comfort.

Angela Carter

Biographical Note

Géza Csáth
(1887–1919)

Csáth was born in Szabadka, then part of the Austro-Hungarian Empire, now a town in northern Yugoslavia. His close, harmonious family suffered its first tragic loss with the premature death of Csáth's mother when he was only nine. The center of the family became the father, a lawyer and respected member of the town's intelligentsia, who later brought a young and unloved stepmother into the home. Csáth hoped to become a painter, as is suggested in "Souvenir," but his father, an amateur musician, wanted him to become a concert violinist. Father and son often played the classics together. The atonality and asymmetrical rhythmic combinations of his son's own compositions were, however, not appreciated by the older Csáth, for whom modern music stopped at Grieg.

Indeed, Csáth showed remarkable talent in several of the arts. While in high school, he published miniature portraits of composers in the local papers, and was sixteen when his first short story appeared in print. Nevertheless, he decided to study composition. Only after his rejection by the Academy of Music did he embark on a more practical career, enrolling in the Budapest Medical School. In the one completed chapter of a novel that was to have had many autobiographical details, he tells of his arrival in Budapest and the move into his first rented room.

After receiving his degree in general medicine, Csáth specialized in neurology and, as a particularly promising young scientist, he was invited to work with Professor Moravcsik at his famous clinic. He spent three years in clinical research

(1910–1913), during which time he published a major monograph, "On the Psychic Mechanism of Mental Disorder." Simultaneously, he contributed to the most important literary journals of the period and became a recognized music critic, one of the first to appreciate the work of Bartók and Kodály. His talents suffered, however, from the paralyzing effects of opium addiction. He started smoking opium in 1909 and by the spring of 1910 was injecting ever larger dosages of morphium and pantopon.

Fewer than a hundred stories, a couple of plays, and a slim volume containing his music reviews are the entire yield of 1908–1912, his years of accomplishment. In 1913 he left the clinic and became a country doctor. Escape from the capital made it possible for him to indulge in opium without the restraint of family and friends, whom he also shocked by a sudden marriage to a young woman disapproved of by all. The following passage from the diary of that period describes his struggle with opium:

In combating myself I can only report one bloody defeat after another. Not even in this respect is fortune willing to smile at me. The week started well with daily quantities of 0.044 and 0.046 which I divided into 3–4 portions. But yesterday and today I reached again that awful vicious circle which is the source of the most shameful remorse. The trouble always starts with not having the strength to wait for my mid-morning stool. Because when I succeed in doing this, and the morphium leaves the intestines, then it is followed by a pleasant, all-day-long hunger which can be satisfied with the regular amount. But if the first sin takes place in the morning, still in bed or before the bowel movements, the same amount doesn't work properly, and causes no euphoria. To commit sin, to harm myself without enjoying it, this is the bitter thought tormenting me. If I had a gun near me, at times like this, I would blow my brains out, right away. . . .

28

At times like this I smoke one cigarette after another until I no longer feel the taste of the smoke. I eat oranges till I get tired of them. Disgusted, I play the piano. I wash. Visit Olga. Find life insufferable. I make an effort to entertain her, but I lack the true sexual interest, and, therefore, I am just getting bored there. To make my stay bearable I put in 0.02–0.03 in the toilet, hating it. This is followed after dinner by 0.02, then 0.01 and 0.01 again. The last one under the pretext that it already belongs to tomorrow's portion. . . . This is an immeasurably loathsome and despicable life. I am so disgusting, weak and pitiful that I have to wonder why Olga still loves me, and hasn't become unfaithful to me. That my weak and forever veiled voice, my steady staring in the mirror, my cynical and shrunken penis, my drawn face, my witless conversation, my impotent, lazy life, my suspicious behavior, my insolence with which I lengthily disappear into the WC, my stupidity, haven't disgusted her yet, for ever and ever. I also think that I stink, because with my sense of smell impaired, I can no longer smell the stench of my poorly-wiped asshole or the mouth-odor caused by my rotting teeth.

His addiction notwithstanding, Csáth served in World War I. In the war and its aftermath, not only did the monarchy collapse, bringing about a major political shift in Central Europe, but with it an entire way of life disappeared, a way of life depicted by Musil, Kafka, and Hašek, which was also the milieu of Csáth and his characters. By the time he was discharged, Csáth was not only physically ill but showed signs of insanity. He carried knives and had his family followed by detectives. Finally, in the presence of their infant daughter, he shot his wife with a revolver. He was moved to an insane asylum where he tried, unsuccessfully, to commit suicide. Months later he was able to escape, and made a last desperate effort to reach Budapest, bound possibly for Dr.

Moravcsik's clinic. At the new demarcation line, near his birth-place, Szabadka, he was stopped by Serbian border guards. After a short struggle he gave up; then, with the bewildered soldiers looking on, he suddenly swallowed poison and died. He was thirty-one. In accordance with Csáth's wishes, his brain, heart, and liver were taken to a Budapest clinic for examination.

Marianna D. Birnbaum

Opium and
Other Stories

The Magician's Garden

I recognized that pair of slender fellows as they came through the station gate into the square.

—The Vass boys!

We walked towards town, enjoying the mild June afternoon. We'd been inseparable through high school, but four years had gone by since we'd graduated and I'd not seen them—they were studying abroad. Our chance meeting pleased them.

Their faces hadn't yet hardened into men's: fine noses and lively clever eyes showed a still-developing intelligence. Their manners were as gentle and charmingly worldly as ever: extraordinary in high-school boys yet somehow attractive to all of us too.

We passed down the main street and into the square. They were hurrying, they had only two hours.

—As a matter of fact, the older Vass boy said, we only came to look at the magician's garden.

—Magician's garden? Where is that? I said.

—You wouldn't know it. We never told anyone about it in those days. Come on with us, you'll see. It's not very far....

We turned off towards the church, crossing the park. Our old dogmatics prof was planted on his old bench, nose in some text. We hailed him. He waved back fondly. We went round back of the church, and I followed them into a dead-end street I'd never noticed before. It was narrow, perhaps two hundred paces long. Odd, but I'd never seen houses like these in my town: low, crudely built, the shape of their windows, the moldings and style of their doorways and gates were archaic somehow. In the street old men and pale, sad-faced women sat on stools and little benches. Tiny girls watered and swept the walks. No sign of wheel tracks anywhere.

At the last house we halted. Actually, the house wasn't visible—only the fence, a high wooden fence, unpainted and so closely slatted you couldn't stick your hand through. You had to put your eye to it to see through. Suddenly I was struck by the heavy fragrance of flowers. On the other side there was a garden about the size of a small room, a plot of ground raised by fill to the height of our belts. And full of flowers.

A special, luxuriant flora. Long-stemmed, with horn-shaped flowers whose petals were like black velvet. In one corner, a bush like a lily, arrayed with giant white blossoms like goblets. And scattered through that garden, thin-stemmed plants with white flowers marked by a single pink petal. It seemed that these gave off that exotic sweetness that cloyed and choked. In the midst of it all a bunch of fat crimson flowers lay tumbled, their silky, fleshy blossoms dipping down among the long stems of furious green grasses. This small, magical plot seemed a kaleidoscope. Just in front of my eyes purple irises bloomed up. A myriad fragrances mingled in its dazzling scent, and every hue of the rainbow glowed from those flowers.

Beyond this garden squatted a small house, two green-shuttered windows opening almost on the ground. No door to be seen. A gabled roof above the windows. There should be a large attic in there. I could see blue carnations beside

the windows. We stared in at this ten-by-ten magic realm silently. Perhaps four minutes passed.

The younger Vass said: This is the magician's garden.

—And the magician lives in there, the other added.

—The thieves live there, too.

—Who? I asked.

—Thieves. His followers and slaves.

—They go out stealing in town. They go just around now, through tunnels. They come out under the roofs of the churches and slide down the bell ropes. They hide little oil lamps under their brown cloaks, they carry masks, daggers and pistols in their belts.

—They sneak into houses, or climb through open windows. They use small picks to get up through dark windows into second stories—it takes them two seconds.

—And then they slip into closets.

—Nobody notices them. They scrunch down among the clothes between boxes. They light their tiny lamps. They wait quietly.

—They wait till everyone's asleep. Then they come out of hiding, stalk through the rooms, break the locks, cut off the children's heads, and leave their daggers in the fathers' hearts.

—And take the treasure back to the magician.

The boys told the secrets of the magician's lair as though reciting an ancient, forgotten poem. Meanwhile, our eyes peered in at the garden.

—Can you guess what's going on in there right now? the younger Vass asked.

His brother replied for me.

—Behind the shuttered window is the bedroom of the thieves. A low, rough-walled shed. A little lamp flickering on the wall, six straw pallets on the right, six on the left. On one side of the floor six robbers sleeping huddled up: their faces can't be seen.

—On the other side, six empty places.

—The thieves are on their way underground to their bloody work.

—When they wake up, they have to crawl out, because you couldn't stand up in such a low place.

—Then the magician feeds them. As if, with his evil dark eyes, he's saying: Go on, stuff it in and bring me bags of treasure, silver and gold.

—The thieves eat fresh lizards and frogs, and for an appetizer they get aged May-beetles that the magician stores in glass jars in his pantry like preserves.

—Then they have to leave. The magician lights his lantern in a skull, and waits in his room. He stays alert reading, in case his thieves get into a fix.

—Or the dogs and children wake up.

—And when the sky in the east begins to gray, he comes here, lies down in the garden.

—And the flowers all turn into girls. And he rolls around among them....

—Until the thieving slaves come home, hand him the swag, which he stores away in his subterranean warehouse, and they all turn in for sleep. Then the house is quiet, dead until evening.

—None of the neighbors have the least idea who lives in here....

A little while longer we watched the magician's garden in silence. One of the Vass boys glanced at his watch then, and said:

—Our train goes in twenty-five minutes. And he sighed.

—We've got to go, the other one said.

Stars could already be seen in the eastern sky. The street was still as a graveyard: not a soul alive but us.

We started back, walking without a word till we reached the church. The Vass boys gazed ahead musing. We circled the park. Three maids were drawing water from the well. They were prettily shaped and laughing gaily. The two boys smiled at them.

The delirious scent of the magician's flowers was dissipating from their lungs. A cab passed. They whistled for it, said goodbye with a grin, and hopped on. The driver cracked his whip and whirled them off towards the brightly-lit main street.

Paul and Virginia

I'd like to tell you Paul and Virginia's story, but I'm afraid to. Because I know you'll glance at it, and if you were to find a bit of exciting or odd stuff at the end, some staccato dialogue, for instance, which I'd turned in an interesting way, then you might feel like reading the thing through. You wouldn't otherwise. And so I'd like to dress up this story with exotic colors and tell it with a catchy tempo. But that's impossible because I don't see it as exciting stuff, frankly. It's mild, pleasant as a Mendelssohn song, except for the last chords. Furthermore, I happen to be fond of Paul and Virginia. I know them; they're not just anybody; I just couldn't caricature their lives. So I'll tell it straight.

They were cousins, blonde, healthy children. I liked being with either of them, and more so when they were together. From their first step, when they were fat, little things, they loved one another, smiling into each other's big baby eyes with wonder. They'd kiss even when no one urged, Go ahead, Paul, or Virginia, kiss your little cousin. They toddled over the lawn together, played through the long, yellow summer afternoons together in the sandbox; and dusk, coming late that time of the year, after supper, would see them into the house embracing.

All idyllic, nothing to spoil their love's fresh loveliness. Only, by the time they'd slowly grown up there was horrid gossip circulating. It wasn't proper or correct, and so forth. Paul's father said right out that it was wrong for him to be hugging his slim, blue-eyed cousin Virginia all the time, or walking her in the vineyards when the crickets were singing in the night.

It saddened me. I'd never seen a love as pure and straight, without sham pretences, without impediments. Usually, the boy's grown up before love arrives: talking to his girl, he stammers, his breath is short; and the girl prevaricates, not giving up any kisses until late in the game... and not on her lips at that. But Paul and Virginia had loved from childhood, and everyone assumed she'd be his wife. When they were children Virginia would tell provincial relatives or guests, I'll belong to Paul, I'll be Paul's wife.

As I have remarked, they hardly noticed reaching fourteen; they were unaware of days coming and going; they never even supposed anything could be occurring that might separate them—a magnetism secreted in each of them. I think Virginia's mother was clever never to say to her, Don't let Paul kiss you any more—people are whispering nasty things. She said nothing. (I know Virginia's mother: a beautiful woman, fading slowly, sighing deeply now and again.) And it was this that pleased me so; it's fine when a boy and girl remain close—which rarely happens—without the usual, ugly petting.

Virginia never restrained Paul's hand when he took her slim waist, nor did she pull away as he sucked long at her lips. They were never angry with one another, in earnest or in jest: they had no need of that shopworn flame to rekindle their ardency, as so many engaged and married couples do. Paul never praised other girls to make Virginia jealous, and she never gazed into the eyes of other boys in order to make herself more desirable to him.

Gradually everyone conceded it would be stupid and

cruel to separate such a well-matched young couple. Even the family's old doctor, the longest holdout, gave up his stubborn opposition—in the name of the science he'd once sworn to respect—and made no more difficulties. When asked, all he later said was, You have to understand that so far as science is concerned today it's not advisable— but I can't guarantee anything tomorrow! (Guffawing, as usual, at this.)

The time at last came, and they sent their application in: could Paul and Virginia, first cousins, be permitted to marry.

Weeks went by without an answer. Each day the poor children waited for their word. It may be ridiculous to compliment them for it, but they thought of nothing else all day. True, that isn't much of an occupation; and there are some of course who will find it disagreeable that Paul and Virginia cared for nothing but their love. But the permit never came.

Day by day they waned, feverish, tremulant. Anyone could see they were losing weight.

Then Paul's father decided to look after the matter, and put a good deal of money into straightening things out. However, it didn't work: the answer he got was, It can't be done.

All that trouble for nothing.

Why should I give you all the details of their misery? A writer mustn't torture his characters or his readers. True, he could get certain interesting effects if he did; but about some things silence is preferable.

Well, Paul and Virginia couldn't legally be married.

So, that beautiful woman who was slowly fading, sighing deeply now and then—Virginia's mother—went to the person who gave the word in cases like hers. I can't recall now if he was a bishop or a member of the cabinet—and she told him something.

The poor lady was so pale in her black silk. Her black hair was combed back severely—not a strand of gray in it. She really was quite beautiful. Anyone seeing her would think, Well, here is a decent, likable woman who probably keeps her home perfectly and raises model children.

She shook, telling her story, her pale face flushing and burning. Paul and Virginia, she said, weren't really cousins: her lawful wedded husband wasn't Virginia's father.

No lie, this. Virginia's mother, though no one knew it, was an adulteress.

That happened one afternoon at the very end of their vigil. Paul and Virginia had looked desperately at each other when the word came: it was as though they'd been condemned to execution, by a remorseless fate. Wild desires gleamed in their great, lovely eyes. It was then Virginia's mother decided. She told them what sacrifice she would make for them. Virginia sobbed, but accepted. I believe (and there's no reason *I* should be angry at her for it) Virginia would have let her mother go to torture had her own happiness depended on it.

But it all ended well. Spring flourished a fanfare.

They were married one sunny day in May redolent with acacia.

That's all there is to it.

An Afternoon Dream

I said to the maid, Giza, open the shutters and let the yellow curtains down. One falls asleep easier this way. But look in on me every fifteen minutes, and wake me if you find me sleeping: I don't want a headache.

I finished my coffee, snubbed my cigarette, and leaned back on the old wine-plush sofa. I glanced at the clock: ten past two.

I dreamt that afternoon of a mute Countess.

I was galloping on a white stallion towards Baghdad. It was a brilliant summer afternoon. The towers of the city, the strips of cedar and palm groves stretched upward, shimmering, sizzling, fading out in the burning, golden dust of the departing sun. Flowers in the gardens breathed out their last fragrance, and the sighs of the roses floated and crowded my way all mixed with the odors of frankincense and balsam trees. I dug my spurs into my steed's flanks because I wanted to reach the city before sunset. I touched the silk wallet on my belt, filled with gold, stood in the stirrups and breathed deeply. A gorgeously sweet, perfumed and wonderful afternoon. My horse flew me along.

I reached the city just after sunset, left the horse in the care of the ostler, and strolled down to the river. The orange veil of dusk spread over the blue radiance of the sky like the fleeting kiss on a girl's face. Dragonflies zigzagged over the stream, and now and then myriads of mayflies flew past along the bank. They would die before the sun went down. At the shore's edge swam many thousands of dead mayflies. Yesterday's or the day before's dusk had interred them—who could tell.

Here at the bank of the river I met the mute Countess. A wide-brimmed straw hat with flowers on it, a green veil about her shoulders. She wore a light pink makeup. She had on tiny white sandals, black stockings, and a black silk skirt. She looked at the sky languidly with grayish-green, tired eyes. A great and silent wisdom hovered over her finely-cut, small, cold lips. I stepped up to her.

I said, Countess, I've heard it said of you your lips are mute, you cannot speak—but your eyes tell me you possess the greatest wisdom. She stopped, her head tilted to one side. The golden hoops of her turquoise earrings quivered from her chiseled lobes. But she didn't look at me. For a moment only her shoulders swayed slightly, her cold, drowsy eyes emanating a violet-hued light. They trembled: it was as though I'd glimpsed a will-o'-the-wisp.

I said, Countess, I came here to have a kiss from you: I ask you to look into my eyes.

She nodded slowly and looked up at me, sticking her little tongue out from her red, silent lips and licking them. At this instant her eyes were all black, with a tinge of blue. Her gaze penetrated deep into my eyes, down to my heart, running down my spine like a slow shuddering. She shook her head gently, as if she wished to say, Impossible.

I said, Countess, you know all you wish to know because muteness makes a woman omniscient. You know also that I've walked a thousand miles because of you alone; that I was born because of you; and that I must die because

of you. Give me your veil, therefore, and pour one drop of scented oil on my brow.

Her eyes again drifted to the distant sky; in them were reflected old tragedies in colors of cold, grayish-green—her beautiful, slender shoulders inclined forward. Then she took a small crystal phial from her skirt pocket. She wetted her long, white fingers and brushed my forehead with the perfumed oil.

I asked, Do you know me well, Countess?

She nodded twice, suddenly and wickedly.

Are you going to love me?

She nodded again, her lips smiling.

I said to her, That's a lie—you're unable to love.

She remained still; she became serious; she took the green silk veil from her shoulders, handed it to me, and then without looking at me, walked off. I dared not follow her with my eyes. I gazed at the silent mirror of the water and tied the veil around my waist.

The last vibrations of the sun's rays had already vanished from the horizon, and the sky blanketed the earth with a mesmerizing, deep topaz-blue. The moon hadn't come up yet; but Sirius glittered like a huge diamond, and Aldebaran and Antares were glowing like ruby cabochons. Sadly, I thought of the exuberant happiness with which I had raced towards Baghdad just a few hours earlier. Then I walked with the stream.

Soon I came across a boat. I got in, untied its anchor, and lay down in the bottom on my back. The city remained long behind me; but the many tales living there sent their angelic music after me. Glass flutes were warbling, and deep-throated magic violins were playing. It was as though the hearts of youths and maidens were playing loose and tumultuous harmonies. I removed the veil of the Countess from my waist and spread it over me like a shroud.

I said to myself, The journey will be long and dreamless. But now I must kiss the mute Lady's lips.

I thought of my stallion: I had paid one thousand pieces of gold for him, and had now abandoned him forever.

The night grew more and more dark. I traveled between unfamiliar, frightening shores. Tall cliffs rose cold and steep on both sides. The evil spirits who dwell in caves left their hiding, flew after me, held to the boat, fluttering over me. I knew I must not speak, or it would be my end; so I remained quiet, and turned the ring on my finger seven times. Upon which I noticed a light shimmering in the bows of the boat. And then the moon, like a great magic lantern, shot up in the sky.

A mild breeze stirred. I wound the Countess' veil about my neck and sat up. I took out the excellent tobacco I'd bought in Aldsezireh, and smoked. But my heart was anxious, full of uncertainty. I could stay in the boat no longer. I directed it to shore and got out. My road took me over a great meadow of moonlight, through dewy, silken grass.

After a long walk I reached a highway. The road was unfamiliar to me. I looked about.

Suddenly my blood froze.

Behind me, three shadows of me were projected on the ground.

Slowly, with caution, I looked once more. Three shadows! I dared not stir—I felt I was in the grip of some horrible power. Giddy, bewildered, I looked at the moon.

At that moment, the light of the moon moved above in the skies. With dizzying suddenness it ran across the West like a signal light yanked on a wire, and left behind a flashing dazzling streak.

I breathed deep and trembled, and looked around. Now the region seemed very familiar. A milestone shone beside the road, and a silvery, double row of poplars stretched along. There were dark vineyards in great patches along the highway on both sides, and small, blind houses asleep in them. Far ahead a carriage trundled in a dust-cloud of mist. I continued in the opposite direction towards a little chapel that had been built by a prince's wife two hundred years ago for her salvation. Faintly through the open door the light of an eternal flame filtered.

I went slowly up the steps. Before the altar the mute Countess was kneeling. I went in, stopping near the portal. The girl was dressed in a white ballgown, pink roses wilted in her black hair. I tiptoed forward carefully, so that I might glimpse her face. In her right hand she held a little mirror and looked intensely at herself. She saw right off that I was present, but only turned to me later. Her eyes were again black, tinged with blue; but the pale pink rouge was gone from her face, and she was now all white. She hid the mirror and motioned that she had something to say to me. I gave her pencil and paper, and she wrote: I prayed to be able to love you.

I asked, Do you want to love me?

Serious, sad, she nodded yes.

I said, Countess, the truth is you love no one. Neither your father and mother nor your sisters and brothers. Even your dead fiancé, the Prince, you loved only when he was dead.

Abashed, she cast her eyes down and stared before her. Then she smiled up at me, her lips offering me a kiss.

I said, I can't accept your kisses yet because you don't love me. And I don't know if you'll ever be able to.

Again she drew her little mirror out, as though seeking the answer to my question. Then she shrugged, fixed her hair, wet her fingers with her tongue and smoothed her eyebrows. She asked for my arm then.

We left the chapel. The dews of the morning were lifting in mists. The moonlight scattered itself clear white on the trees, the road and on the young woman's face. The sacred force of the earth thrust in powerful, fascinating bursts from the bushes, the grass, the dark, distant oak-forests, spreading everywhere in great waves. It was chill. At a garden gate she stopped and held her hand out. Her cold, small, elastic fingers gripped my burning hand; then she slipped through and latched it. I went on a few paces, but stopped right away. Standing on the crossbar of the fence and holding to the sharp palings, the girl fixed her eyes on me.

Bewildering mischief and gay naughtiness smiled from her. Her mute lips were compressed in a stubborn silence, and the cold moonlight precisely outlined her tangled black hair's shadow over her eyebrows. I stepped closer, and looked into her eyes, amazed, disbelieving, I searched out the concealed rays of her glance.

I said, Countess, you're so beautiful I could stand here a hundred years just looking at you.

Her mute lips curved in a smile, and she waved adieu with her fan. I returned the salute ardently with my hat; whereupon she vanished among the dark boughs of the fruit trees.

In the east the dawn had broken, the black clumps of bushes and trees were separating, pierced by the dim blue light of the morning. I had to rush to the station, and could think of the Countess meanwhile. At that hour I didn't love her because I believed she could never love me. I decided I'd rather forego her kisses. I bought my ticket—I was the sole passenger—and traveled back to Budapest. At the Keleti stop, however, I got into a taxi, and let myself be driven to a magician who lived in Buda. He opened the gate himself.

He said, I knew you'd come. Because of the Countess.

I answered, Yes, I want her more than anything else. I think I'd even like to have a child with her—but her fingers are elastic and cold, the colors of her eyes change, and her heart's cold and wicked.

The magician said, We'll talk about it, and showed me to his room. He sat me down and gazed at me for a long while. Finally he spoke. As yet, no one has seen the Countess weep. But if you ever see her tears, bring some to me, and I'll examine them. He handed me a small crystal box and explained how to keep the tears.

I said goodbye and walked back to Pest over the Chain Bridge. I've had a hard day, very tiring, with work demanding concentration—many empty hours. Noon was warm, dinner without an appetite, a throbbing heart, a drowsy afternoon. I got home towards five. I bathed, shaved, and changed. When I drove to the station, I found the city wonderfully beautiful and pleasant. I felt very happy and young. As though my body were light, nearly weightless. Health and purity had entered my heart; everything I saw about me spoke its name clearly, and was interesting and good.

But once there, I looked for the young woman a long time in vain, on the roads and over the fields: I even went into town. But she wasn't amongst the strollers on the Promenade either. I worried and grew impatient. Only a few hours remained to me, for I wanted to sleep tonight. In the late evening, sadly dejected, I plodded to the station.

And noticed her at a corner, calmly looking off into the distance, leaning forward ever so slightly, a sly, mocking smile on her lips.

I said, You didn't wait for me, Countess. I'm not angry at you though, because I'm aware you don't love me, and never will.

She clung to my neck, offering her mouth.

I asked, Do you imagine this can reward me for having sought you so long? You hid so I'd find your kiss more precious later on. If I took it now I'd be unable to regard you highly, because I'd have to resign myself to the fact that you cannot cry—which is the worst thing that can be said of a beauty. Her face turned to me, rigid and sober. Tiny yellow and red flames danced in her green eyes—it was as though she'd aged twenty years. She signed that she wished to write, and this is what she said: The dead Prince's mother put a curse on my heart when he died, because I hadn't wept for my fiancé.

I said, You must rid yourself of that curse!

Intrigued, she looked at me.

One tear, you must shed one, single little tear for me. And you must never expect *me* to weep over you.

She humbly acquiesced, her head bowed. My heart gave a hot leap: at that moment her face was fresh, young as a girl's. She asked for something to write with: I look into my glass and see my beauty fading.

And it will fade—because you don't like the children you'll bear.

Again she wrote, Never shall I bear a child! and snatched the paper, tearing it to shreds as though regretting what she'd written.

Will you wait for me, Countess, when I come another time?

Nodding, she took a wilted pink rose from her hair and handed it to me. I embraced her tenderly, she inclined to me obediently, leaning her head on my chest. We parted then.

I traveled home. A few weeks passed; the summer passed; and we didn't see one another. To the young woman I wrote saying we must wait until the curse disappears of itself from her hard, cruel heart. She wrote back to say she agreed, and would wait for me gladly, pray, and bathe her feet each Friday, seven times, in warm water reddened by birdblood.

At long last, on a cold bright October afternoon I went to see what had happened to the young woman. She hadn't waited for me; she hadn't kept her promise. I looked for the garden to which I'd escorted her that morning, and jumped the fence. The paths were desolate; dry leaves clattered at my feet; I saw footprints nowhere. Huge peaches and apples still smiled on the trees; yellow and blue clusters of grapes hung fat, overlaying their leaves; and as I moved on, a small yet noble and charming castle revealed itself amongst the trees. All the doors were locked as if the place had been deserted. I walked round the building. On the back face, one green shuttered window on the ground was half open, and I looked in. The Countess sat in her slip near the window, her eyes gazing up at the clouds in the sky, just as I had seen her at first. She stirred, smiled, and passed a chair to me through the window. Calmly I climbed from it into the room. The young woman embraced me, and her clasp was hot and torpid, desirous yet painful, like a migraine. I sat and searched her eyes from a little distance. She stretched her legs which were bare to the knees, and looked at me, touched.

Miss, the time has not yet come. For this small while we should love one another as though I were your son, you my little girl.

With eyes flashing, she signed to me that she'd be good and took my hand. We crossed a series of rooms, all of them dim, finally reaching a double door. She switched a small electric light on and extracted a key from somewhere beneath the threshold. With a sharp crack the lock sprang open. We entered a great hall with mirrored walls. The Countess vanished from my side, but there were hundreds upon hundreds of others instead of her in the mirror. There were so very many, flocks of identical girls milling about and staring at me. Naked. Here, one with raised arms; there, another, her arms behind her: and their eyes all glittered different ways, and their aspects were different, too. I was dizzied, frightened, but decided that since I was there I'd fight courageously. In one corner I chanced upon a portrait of my young lady, who was more attractive to me than all the others. She stood leaning over, her head inclined. Seen from the side, her eyes appeared light blue. I studied them—they were full of tears. I approached nearer: it wasn't a portrait but the genuine Countess. Quickly I took my crystal box out, and when one diamond drop coursed down her cheek I caught it at her chin and carefully tucked it away. We returned to her little room then.

Dusk was near. We must have lost much time unawares in that hall of mirrors. She dressed, arranged her hair, and wrote that she'd accompany me, as her people would come

53

home only in the late afternoon. We went to the station, where I said, I was going right to the magician to have the teardrop examined: everything depended on it. And she wrote: I shall pray that my tear may be good and that my heart may be freed from the curse of the old Princess.

That whole evening her eyes were light blue, and on her face a tinge of deep pink instead of that sad, marble pallor.

As the train moved off with me, and I watched the Countess sadly, sweetly waving at me in the light of a kerosene lantern, I fervently believed her teardrop good. It wasn't, though. I gave it to the magician who tasted it and said immediately he thought poorly of it. Yet he went on to complete the tests according to the formula. He mixed it with different drops of variously-hued liquids. Were the teardrop good, the mixture would turn a translucent white; if not, it would be darkened. In the magician's small testing vial, the mixture went nearly black.

He said, I'm afraid the curse of the old Princess has affected you, too. He looked at me, held the mirror up to me—what I saw was terrible: my brown eyes glittering an uncanny blue.

The magician said gravely, I know much; but only one man in the whole world can undertake your cure—Sinbad, the two-hundred-year-old wizard in Baghdad. Go to him. And hurry.

I left that day. After a long, fatiguing journey of many weeks, I reached Baghdad and recalled the day I'd raced towards the city for the first time, happy and young. When I found Sinbad it was late in the evening. The Sage was bent over a great book, reading by lamplight. He motioned me to a seat, heard me out, and examined my face at some length with his calm, blue, wise eyes. He took his mirror out then and gazed into it intensely. Soon the likeness of the Countess materialized in its smooth dark steel face, faintly at first, then gradually outlined clearly. The Wizard wagged his head: the case was evidently quite serious.

He said, The Countess will weep authentic tears—but only over the bier of her child. Yet how can she have children when she likes no one and carries the curse of sterility? New shoots can never blossom from the frozen flame of her embrace—calm, steady, fertile warmth is necessary for that. And that is what is lacking in those whose eyes change their color, who know themselves and one another too well to feel pure and permanent love. Nevertheless, no other way offers the hope of resolution.

I thanked Sinbad the Magician for his advice. I journeyed home. I married the Countess.

Our first months were horrible. We watched one another's eyes between kisses, examining our faces. We were constantly tempted to think that we were doomed day by day to be robbed of our future happiness by the curse's power.

Often I said, Countess—even afterwards I called her that—we shall perish never having felt the warmth of great and true love though we deserve to have it: we desire no one else, and we want children. If only, as Sinbad the Magician asserted, to have your heart purified by weeping real tears in the pain of death. At such times she would look at me in such a way it seemed that were she then to weep, her tears must be good.

The child came during a winter of ruthless cold and blizzards. The child for whom we'd so yearningly waited, and who we knew must die because of us. Through her hard hours of suffering, the Countess' lips remained mute, and even though she'd mistrusted it to the last moment, her little anxious face was lit by a ray of hope.

The child was born. So beautiful was he that we gazed at him amazed for hours on end. Anxious, fearful, we kept vigil over his dreaming, planning to part forever, giving up our own happiness to save the child from death. The Countess, however, wished to nurse it herself, agreeing to divorce after she had weaned it. Awful days dawned for us once more. The nights were worse. I often woke to see the Countess seated by candlelight at her mirror, looking at her eyes. She was wondering if she could weep. In mute despair she bent over me when I asked her why she never slept. Misery! We were indeed cursed!

And the child grew, becoming more beautiful; while we suffered, waiting, not knowing what to do.

High summer had come when I woke at daybreak to the Countess' shriek. She held the child in her arms. And she put it down before me on the bed.

The little body was cold, lifeless.

I said, He's died. If you can cry, now's the time. And desperately added, Cry.

She blushed, staring at the tiny corpse. I jumped up, dressed, and went to order the coffin.

At noon I came home. The Countess gazed at the child, her eyes tearless. I came home at night. The Countess' eyes were dry. I said then, We must take the child to be buried tonight. This is our duty.

She nodded and quickly changed into black. We hired a carriage, conveyed the coffin secretly down the dark stairway, and drove off with it on our knees. The night was starless, pitch. All around us the vast meadows mutely listened. Silent, rigidly mute, we stared out, submerged in nervous grief held back. I don't know how long we traveled on like that. Quite abruptly, and unexpectedly, our way was barred by a river. We stopped, sent the carriage away, got into a boat. I released the rope. Down the river the boat swam swiftly. The Countess' pale face, her white fingers clasped, began to be faintly visible in the darkness. Between strange and frightening shores the water carried us. High, steep cliffs flanked us. The evil spirits who lived in the caves flew forth, following after us, clinging to the boat and fluttering around us. Seven times I turned the ring on my finger. Soon a weak light rose low in the sky. And then, like a great magic lantern, the moon mounted to the heavens. I steered the boat to shore; we climbed out, carrying the coffin on foot. After traversing a great distance we reached a highway. It was an unfamiliar road. Gigantic bats flittered constantly over our heads. Horror stroked our spines with its iced fingers, and we shivered ... And I saw that in this moonlight each of our forms cast a triple shadow: I had three, and the Countess three. But the little coffin had no shadow at all.

I said, Let's stop. We must dig a grave. With our nails, since we have no other tools.

We knelt on the earth and went to work. I don't know how long we dug. It was darkening by the time the hole was ready: the air was frozen, and it was snowing. The flakes covered our shoulders, our backs, and settled on the Countess' hat like a wreath.

I said, Now we can bury the coffin. Slowly, we let the little black box down.

At that moment, the Countess' eyes began shedding tears. Thousands upon thousands of diamonds, those drops seemed pouring down on the coffin. The snow lay melting in the pit, the soil grew wet and soft, and sighed. In a few minutes, I had filled in the grave. I straightened up. I went to the Countess and embraced her. Her lovely, mute lips parted gently, and in her kiss I felt the curse upon us no longer.

I said, We'll start our life again. She nodded happily, and we set out for home in the cold, snowing night.

The voice of the cheerful, slender maid called, Time to get up, Sir!

I couldn't open my eyes. A deadly fatigue held me to my sofa. And a headache, with its tickling, dull pain, lurked in the nape of my neck.

What time is it, Giza?

Nearly two-thirty.

Saturday Evening

Saturday evenings—oh those are always the nicest. No hot meal, meat and vegetable and noodle pudding one after the other—but lots of other things. And, we can eat whatever we like. Also tea that Grandma brews in the big brass samovar on the little table beside the cupboard; or else eggs, and we have to tell our cook Éva how many we'd like. Or we can have the tiny canned fish Father brings home. The whole thing's simply wonderful. There's a platter of toast on the table, a dish of butter and cream cheese, and a bowl of boiled potatoes.

Even Father and Mother seem happier those evenings. And they'd rather eat supper like this—that's what I think anyway—it's much nicer and better than the usual one all week long.

Grandma drinks only tea then. She makes it the color of wine, and while it's steeping she burns rum with sugar in her cup. The rum browns with little pinkish-purple flames now and then flickering above the edge of the cup, and Grandma takes her glasses off, watching, smiling, and rubbing sugar cubes on a lemon. Father eats fish first, but then asks for green pepper, salt, pepper, mustard, caraway, capers and parsley. He takes some of each, adds a lot of cream cheese and butter, and stirs it all together with the heavy silver spoon. It's delicious spread on toast. Peter and I both take turns eating everything. Mother gives us whatever we ask for, and then Father says, I don't care, but the kids'll get sick, and then Mother pleads for us, Don't worry. I'm watching.

After supper Father smokes. I bring him his pipe from the corner, Peter the matches from the chest, and Anna the humidor. Slowly Father stuffs his big, carved meerschaum and lights it. It sends up gorgeous blue rings, three for each of us: for me, Anna and Peter, and one for Grandmother and Mother, too, if we ask. Then he reads the paper. Mother takes *Olajág* from the cabinet and reads. Grandma scurries to the kitchen with the pantry-keys.

Soon Juli comes in with hot water in the basin. We have to wash our feet. Anna's usually first. (We make her believe that girls must wash their feet first.) Juli soaps our feet, tickling, scrubbing and rinsing them really clean. Meantime she tells us three stories: Ironhead, the Seven Ravens, the Witches. The best one's about the Witches.

Father and Mother are in the parlor. They take lamps and open the piano. Father plays and Mother sits beside him. They chat, and Father kisses Mother now and then.

While Juli tells the stories I listen to the music, too, because I know them both. The music's very sad; only Father and Mother like it. We don't. But if he plays something merry, we jump and dance on our beds. (Once the springs broke; but it wasn't on a Saturday, because we wouldn't have been spanked if it had been.)

Later Juli carries the basin out and mops up the puddle on the floor. We're dozing by then. But it's bad falling right asleep. We keep our eyes open because the Sandman hasn't come yet, and anyway we can't sleep well till he comes. Besides, it would be a pity to when everything's so beautiful. The dining-room lamp throws a little light into ours because we have the door half-closed. We can hear the piano clearly.

But soon Grandma comes in. She lays the keys on the cup-board and pours water in the pitcher to make sugarwater. We can hear her taking the cubes from the bowl. We can hear them plopping into the pitcher: one, two, three, four, five, six, seven. (That's how many she usually drops.) She stirs it with a spoon and brings some to each of us in bed, careful that none of us gets more than the others.

Now it's time for sleep. Grandma goes to her room and starts undressing. The kitchen door opens and Juli comes out with a decanter and glasses on a tray. She crosses the rooms; the glasses tinkle against one another; she puts the tray on the table; goes out again. Minutes later she returns with the nightlight. This she takes to Father's room and sets it on the table.

At that moment the Sandman's here.

When we showed him, Father said it was the decanter's shadow. And when in fact he took the decanter away, the Sandman vanished too. Yet it's no shadow, it's the Sandman. He's like an owl and he seems to sit on the edge of Father's bed. It's horrible looking at him, because he's huge, he's ugly and frightening. We pull our blankets up over our ears right away. We hardly ever drop the corner of our blankets and peek out for just a second. The Sandman's standing there still, waiting for us to fall asleep. And we really do have to sleep, because he wants us to.

When you think about it, it's impossible to guess where the Sandman could be in the daytime. That nobody knows. One thing's sure enough: even the Sandman's jollier on Saturday evening. Next day's Sunday after all; we sleep later then, and he likes that. He likes people to sleep a lot. When we feel as if there's sand in our eyes at night and our eyelids are growing heavier and heavier—the Sandman's doing that. Most likely he's got something to do with yawning too.

. . . In the parlor my parents are slowly getting ready. They shut the piano, put out the lights, and come to the bedroom slowly, embracing. I can clearly hear it minutes after when Father pours himself water, sets the decanter down, and drinks.

Afterwards the Sandman stretches out on the wall, looming larger and larger—everybody must sleep now, is what that means. Father says, Tomorrow morning I'll buy the cauliflower myself at the market.

Mother answers something, but nobody can hear what she's saying now. Then Father goes through all the rooms with a candle. He checks the locks on the door and comes back. He snuffs the candle and goes to bed too. Everyone's in bed by then. The Sandman, the giant Sandman, crouches on the edge of the bed by the wall, watching.

Trepov on the Dissecting Table

Two white-jacketed orderlies were prepping a short, blonde corpse. The big, marble-topped dissecting table could have taken a fellow twice his size. Just a couple of days ago this flaccid cadaver, stocky and short as a boy, was still known as Trepov. Known everywhere simply as Trepov.

The two men worked cheerfully and quickly. They sponged the flesh over again, letting the bloodied water run down the drain cut in the table top. Then they seized the corpse by its shoulders, heaved it to a sitting posture, and sponged off the fat, white back. One took a comb out and ran it through the blonde hair. But he parted it on the wrong side, not as the dead man had done when among the living.

—Vanya, said the older one, he didn't wear his hair like that. Part it on the right side.

But Vanya, who seemed unusually cheery today—from time to time whistling through his teeth—replied that everything would be done the way he, Vanya, liked it.

Then they lifted the washed and dried body in their arms and carried it to the next room. There it was clothed in linen, stockings and good shoes, and a gold-trimmed uniform.

Gazing at the medals, the older man was touched. And though it was rather unusual for an orderly in a dissecting room—and, strictly speaking, quite forbidden—he began philosophizing.

—What good's all this done for him? He can go right to hell with them now.

—That's why he was awarded them, Vanya replied. So he could end up like this. All we need is for these gentlemen to be dying in bed. Oh no, we're going to slit your bellies and stuff them with straw to keep you from dripping. Vanya began speechifying thunderously—What do you think, Uncle Nicolai, how many more Russians would be walking the earth today if this pig'd croaked a year ago?

This question was followed by a pause because they had to struggle with the collar. The older man answered when they'd finally got it fixed.

—If not this one, there'd have been another. Listen, Vanya, the Little Father needed a man like him, because if he'd been any different the Little Father would have sent him packing and hired someone else.

Vanya wasn't swayed by this logic. He swore bitterly. The dead man was a pig. On account of him, more people were murdered than absolutely necessary.

They finished the dressing. The older man lit his pipe then, examined the costume, adjusting all those gilt-enameled medals, drawing the cuffs out just so from the sleeves, and folding the arms across the breast. Then they laid the stiff on a felt-covered iron cart. The older man opened the door to the corridor to wheel it out.

But Vanya suddenly shut it again.

—Why'd you close it when I want it open? asked the older man.

—Just a second, Uncle Nicolai. I still need something.

—What's that?

—You'll see. Vanya tiptoed around the room, glancing back towards the dissecting room, too. Then he came back to the corpse, raised his arm—and slapped the face hard, three times.

The two men stared in silence at each other.

Vanya said, Yes, if I hadn't humiliated this murdering son of a bitch, I'd be a cur. There isn't a worse bastard rotting in hell. It was a good chance to. . . .

The older man nodded. Bolder, the younger man smiled back.

—Sure, I hit this pig. Now I'll kick him! Excited, he got up, balancing himself on the cart and, careful not to soil the dampened uniform, kicked at the face as hard as he could. Then he hopped down. The older man had the sponge ready. They rewashed the face, combed the head. Their laughter was low and tense. They dropped the subject. They began to roll the cart towards the door. The older man started to open it.

—Hold it—just once more!

With all his strength, he slapped the corpse's face again. Now we can go, he stammered, his face flushed with the thrill of it.

After delivering the body, they paced in silence to the dissecting room. Then Vanya said, You know, Uncle Nicolai, if I hadn't done that, it would've troubled me for the rest of my life. Imagine, what a chance! May God damn my soul if that wasn't the right thing to do!

—Good for you, the older man said soberly.

When Vanya got into bed that night, he rubbed his palms with pleasure, thinking how proud his son—whom his wife was then expecting—how proud the lad would be when he grew up and heard the story of that day's doings. Wonderful. The brat's big, dark eyes would open wide, and he'd stare at him almost as though he were a god.

But he didn't think much longer about it, for he was soon fast asleep, breathing evenly, deeply, like all healthy people.

Erna

Erna was of course from Budapest.

A homely creature, her girlfriends remarked. And Erna was considered truly plain. The boys saw *something* in her, however, and there were days when they said, What an oddly lovely little face! But they said it only to themselves, and besides Erna seldom had such good days. On the whole she wasn't pretty, she wasn't lovely, and she wasn't charming. Erna knew it only too well, and in fact she thought herself even homelier, more unattractive and unalluring than her girlfriends did.

There was one thing though, one single thing about her that unfailingly drew connoisseurs to her: her smell—or more literarily, her fragrance. Her hair and her neck radiated a divine scent. Once Astalos, a sardonic fellow just admitted to the bar, getting a whiff and being thoroughly absorbed by this perfume, said to himself, I don't care if she's homely or pretty once in a blue moon or her dowry's practically nil—I'd marry her anyway... if her ankles were just half an inch thinner and her feet a few sizes smaller!

I might note that Astalos could have dared to disregard her ankles and feet: Erna's scent was actually marvelous enough to have compensated any man for whatever lack of feminine qualities. Astalos couldn't see it, though someone else did. Erna's piano teacher, a pleasant man with good taste and more experienced with women than Astalos, knew that having several good qualities in a woman is unimportant: face, figure, voice, manners, and style of dress are inessential. What's crucial, let it even be one of the foregoing, is that she have at least *one* good feature, and it had better be an important one.

This serious bespectacled man silently inhaled Erna for an hour a day for several weeks. At the end of the month he proposed—when the hour was over.

Erna ran through the usual program first. She played a Czerny *étude*, some of the *Études for Forty Days*, and a few exercises of Bernini that she never got right. She'd stop playing, shrug and pretend to be an untamable filly, Salome the future demon—she knew, in short, how to handle men. But let me describe how the hour went. Next came a few of Bach's *Two Part* and *Three Part Inventions*. These she managed better. Now Erna displayed her knack at counterpoint. She overemphasized the dominant voice, drowning the other out.... But then, one knows how women play the piano when they want to demonstrate their superior intellect.

Bach was followed by a few Chopin pieces. Now Erna pedaled, cheating, doing away with whole passages and taking off at fast tempi. Not even the devil could have handled her. The piano teacher, Stefan Balla, interrupted her, rapping, but to no avail—Erna played the "Waltz" through to the end. It never occurred to Balla that of course he should have slapped Erna's hands and it would all have been taken care of. Modern teaching methods, even in music, permit no striking—and Balla was a modern pedagogue.

At the hour's end he proposed.

Erna felt the time had come to make up for all her bitter days of lacking self-confidence, the many disappointing hours before the mirror that added up to so much suffering for this basically gentle, hence terribly vain, woman. It was clear to her from the first instant what she had to do: turn Balla down! Regardless of who he might be, even if he were the number one man in town—even then.

—No, she said, it's impossible, my dear friend, quite impossible. I'm sorry. And she shrugged as though meaning to say she wasn't to blame and had no idea how she'd placed herself in such an awkward position.

In fact, she wasn't to blame for anything. Erna had set out to achieve everything but someone's falling in love with her. What mattered to her was having her girlfriends say she was an "odd girl." What also mattered to her was that her mother, a nice, plump woman, should remark, Erna's quite the madcap! It was also her desire that her German governess declare to her gossips: *Ich kann's nicht mit Ihr aushalten!* But she never tried to please. Her odd behavior is explained by the fact that she lived in constant apprehension that someone might say, Well, well, even this homely girl wants to be loved!

She resolved that sentence in her mind, and it was unbearable. We can understand her whole character by it. It was the reason she refused to converse at length with boys who attracted her at parties; why she'd run off rudely; why she'd kiss her girlfriends so passionately, pinching them too till she drew blood. The fear of being rejected made this woman what she was. It was the reason why poor Balla, with his fine, inquisitive nose and handsome forehead—which only a man over thirty has—with his pleasant gray eyes and clean-shaven face, had to slip out of Erna's house unnoticed.

And Erna sighed in relief: she felt like jumping out of her

skin. She grinned; she laughed aloud; she looked at herself in the mirror and, singing, stuck out her tongue so that the two of them, the real Erna and her reflection in the glass, touched. Who cares about Balla, wandering off on Andrássy Boulevard, his nose full of Erna, his heart full of pain! The point was that now she had realized what she'd never believed in or hoped for: there was one who loved her, who would have married her.

From then on Erna swiftly grew pretty. The desire slowly grew in her to spend more time trying on shoes and dresses. Fewer and fewer people used the word "sloppy" for her, and not often. In short, Erna saw to it that her blouse and skirt were fastened perfectly; moreover she even adjusted her skirts before the mirror according to the law of symmetry. A shoemaker of genius fashioned a pair of gorgeous shoes for her. When Astalos saw Erna's ankles in these shoes, he said, I don't know what's happened to that girl. They must have given her new legs or fixed her old ones. I don't know, but as she is now the girl's attractive and deserves the attention of the most particular of men.

Needless to add, Astalos included himself among "the most particular of men," and began courting Erna—on the banks of the Danube, at the skating rink, at the Gerbaud, etcetera, Budapest style. (Jesus Christ, but Life's shallow!) Within two weeks Astalos was wonderfully rejected. Erna needed that for her self-confidence, and so the girl sacrificed—with a sure instinct—a marriage which in other respects would have been quite adequate.

It's worth remarking that Astalos was trying to seduce Erna while proposing to her: being an adherent of the modern school, he held to the principle that one should only marry a girl one knows down to the last details.

Erna didn't hold back in that game—she liked Astalos—but when it came to marrying him she said, No.

After Astalos two or three more young men suffered the same fate. Erna didn't boast of it. She didn't want to make her girlfriends envious; she wished merely to rehabilitate herself, for her own sake. And she accomplished that. What would have happened if, in addition to nature's other stinginess, Erna had lacked even that *one* compensation? The answer's easy: 1) Balla would never have proposed, so there'd have been no refusal; 2) lacking self-confidence, Erna would have neglected her looks even more and would never have sought out her master cobbler who had created the previously mentioned precious shoes for her; 3) on that premise Astalos' and the others' offers wouldn't have been forthcoming; 4) Erna would have remained forever an intolerable creature with frequent attacks of the spleen, as she had been before; 5) the whole affair would have deteriorated further when Erna passed twenty, and things would have been in even worse shape; 6) Erna would have felt herself growing burdensome to her family and begun resenting them and planning a trip abroad; 7) they wouldn't have let her go, she would have wept a lot and ceased speaking to her father and mother for weeks on end; 8) Father and Mother then secretly present her with a fiancé (30,000—not bad!)—Erna talks about her fiancé only with the most intense disgust, but the wedding comes off anyhow; 9) Erna begins talking divorce by the second month of the marriage, whereupon she is promised a slap in the face; 10) at the close of the second year, she delivers a baby girl. She's a wretched housekeeper, an incompetent mother, and an impatient, nagging shrew of a wife. She drives her husband away from home and he turns in his sorrow to cards and etcetera etcetera. In other words, Erna's life might have turned out as just described.

We know, however, that it happened differently on account of a slight but most significant accident. The moral of this story, with its ancillary combinations, is that our fate is indeed directed by small accidents. The happiness or unhappiness of our entire life may depend on accident, on small fortuitous circumstances. Erna, the intolerable nasty girl who was always like a bitter grimace or a string out of tune, disturbing and dissonant, turned out a charming, well-balanced young woman.

I think whoever marries her will do quite well.

The Surgeon

I noticed the surgeon the first time I went to that seedy café on the edge of the town. His one black coat was threadbare, though clean. A scraggly, graying chestnut mustache and large, deepset eyes suited his pale face. His watery eyes glittered with the light of café nights. He spoke softly, almost whispering, as doctors consulting do. During the most casual of conversations, over a piece in the newspaper with one of the customers, say, he would gaze into the other's eyes. As though taking a special interest in him. His opinion was always delivered in periods too, like instructions to a patient. I was impressed by the aristocratic demeanor of this shabby man, just as I have been by the faded, fine velvets one sees in the antique chateaux of ancient nobility.

—Who is that gentleman? I asked the garçon.

—A doctor. Surgeon once. Been coming over a year now.

He heard me calling for one of the medical papers one time, and approached me. Lauded the profession, inquired about the university. We chatted a bit, and he showed himself to be learned. I was particularly struck by some psychosomatic views I'd never read before. I was fascinated by his insights and the imaginativeness which he invested even trivial matters with in talking about them. It surprised me to see how he'd adapted to circumstances, compromised with his life—he even seemed at ease in it. We had our coffee and I left. (I was still in a hurry in those days.)

Once I stopped by late at night. He sat alone, drinking.

Eyes shut, he raised the absinthe to his lips with such desir-ous seeking, draining the green syrup so slowly and plea-surably that I realized the surgeon was alcoholic. More, that he was a confirmed, passionate drunk, lost and drifting steadily towards the DT's. In that moment I was hit by the odd glint in his eyes, the disinterested gaiety and hairsplitting sharp intellect: the man must once have been very different. Alcohol's transmogrified him.

He started, seeing me. I saw he was mortified by my presence, a colleague's. He asked me over. I ordered an absinthe for myself, which relieved him. In a little while I felt the beginnings of a bit of soul-baring; in ten minutes he was deeply into it.

—After all, my friend, what's most important in life? Why do we suffer? Why do we eat? Why do we love? Why is a man joyful? Because of life. How ridiculous, when life comes suddenly to a halt, and that's it. But why? What pre-vents a scientist from completing his work, an artist from exploring his ideas, fathers from seeing their children to maturity? I know why. It's quite simple: why does time move on? That's the basic question.

Listen, and I'll tell you. In the first place, time doesn't move—we do. That's been accepted for a long time—Kant knew all about it. There is no such thing as time. But we do have a solid point of reference: we know our body deteriorates, our brain atrophies, sickness kills... time exists. As I've said, however, there's no such thing as time.

Next question: where did we get this killjoy perspective from?

Well, it's no more than a temporary phase in the devel-opment of the brain. Embryology offers a wealth of analogy. It so happens that when Man stepped out of the primeval monkey world, he left Nature behind. His brain evolved tremendously. Unbeknownst to us, he picked up attitudes that put himself and the world into a new, shall we say more sophisticated, perspective. Perhaps this new outlook is what destroyed Man's psychic happiness. Perhaps it's what put the concept of time into his head. Perhaps this new perceptual dimension, relatively imperfect as it is although absolutely higher—and certainly a mere temporary capacity—is what makes us suppose that it's time that's passing. But that's all temporary, as I say. No need to expound on it: evolutionary phases pass very, very slowly. So we've reached this point: time weighs heavy on the human race. And that's why we're assaulted by degeneration, by trouble and pain, and death.

Now that's a serious problem indeed. Time's poison filters into our philosophy, our art, our ordinary conversation. It's Man's twin as soon as he leaves childhood, and stays with him until his life ends. Schopenhauer writes *The World as Will and Idea,* Shakespeare says, "To be or not to be." We can be grateful to time for the *Fifth Symphony*— Beethoven's Fate Symphony—in which we can hear in that *danse macabre* theme, all its seconds pouring inexorably away like sand. And all that says no more than what every man banally sighs aloud: Well, well, we're getting old! Banal.

And here's my proof. I said, the concept of time becomes the damned goggles of our mind only after childhood. It's true, really: time's passage doesn't disturb the child. Not merely because his body's resilient and strong and his thoughts occupied otherwise, but primarily because his spiritual development's much lower. It stands to reason: in the embryo the circulation of the future human being's blood's quite simple, it's got gills—in other words, it recapitulates the species' preceding evolutionary stages. But arriving here, this crudity—imperfection, let's call it, looking at it from the race's viewpoint—disappears, because it merely expedites the journey to the stage today's adult stands at, relatively speaking. But evolution has still to take off from that. The time's coming when Man will have reached the same level of development today's child is at, even the full-grown man of today—while still an embryo. And this spiritual embryonic stage is exactly the same as the child's ignorance of time! But look at the stage when his psyche's already developed and we see that time has already woven its net over his brain. He can never rid himself of it. In the European this stage comes between fourteen and twenty. It's easy to visualize a day coming when man will pass through this period in childhood while still an embryo. That will be the day! Till then, what can you do... we're stuck here. Medical science is destined to save the human race from this physical affliction, this suffering. The question is crucial today because people are more than ever before obsessed with time. Not even the struggle of making a living can distract Twentieth-Century Man from this piteous insanity.

We've got to do something about it, sir. In cases with similarly excruciating pathological or physiological phenomena surgery doesn't have to stand by with its arms folded. If this time-craziness never existed before but does now, then it's obviously located in the center of the brain. But that's merely a hypothesis I don't need anyway, because here's where I stand: I'm the man who can scientifically demonstrate that this substratum of the soul's development actually is a substratum. I can prove it. I shall find its seat in the brain. I'll stress the possibility of surgical intervention, its necessity. Finally I make the procedure public: I perform the operation and await the judgment of science on my results.

I have found time in the brain. It doesn't differ externally from an ordinary brain cell. Yet it's the nucleus of misery, sickness, the senseless sorrow of passing on. It can be quantitatively greater in one man than another. It elaborates its appendages, its branches and forks like a polyp into the fresh and healthy brain—hence into every aspect of our thoughts.

Of course, this is a great task for the surgeon, but it's absolutely simple. All we have to know is what to cut. I know it. And I'll offer my discovery to the man who wishes above all to be rid of time, who is borne down by the idea of passing on. Him I shall help.

I'll rent a huge operating theater. It will be jammed with observers. In its center we set up the operating table. Three assistants make preparations. The aristocrats of finance and science crowd the hall, mingling with the poor. Finally, silence. I put on my gown; I'm helped into my rubber boots. Calmly I scrub up and give the order: Start the anesthesia! I tie the apron around me and pull on my gloves. Is he out? Good! Blood pressure? Fine! I touch his head. Slowly I make my incision from the base of the skull to the parotid. The audience watches, holding its breath. Binoculars are trained on me. I stop the bleeding. I peel back scalp and muscles in an area about half a palm's size. Raspatory for the periostal! I have now reached bone. Auger, please! Trepanation. I have made the hole... I am at the *dura mater*. I carefully cut the membrane, fold it aside. With my fingers I penetrate one of the folds, the one I alone know—and extract time.

And as easily as that I just spoon out this evil hornet's nest of human grief. In a few minutes the whole thing's finished. I hand the time cells round in a dish. Then I sew up the arachnoid, the *pia mater* and *dura mater*, and reset the pieces of skull-bone I've cut out... tying up the veins. Stitch the scalp, muscles and skin, and dress the wound. I am all done. I waken the fellow. (Here the surgeon rose from his chair and continued almost shouting.) This is the man of the future, the really new man who's able to solve today's secrets and tomorrow's truth with his fresh clean brain. He has total recall because facts don't pass away for him—they line themselves up as equal powers in his consciousness. The audience applauds wildly. I remove my surgical gown and take my bows in my dove-gray morning attire. The happiness of mankind addresses me, jubilant. In three days' time the wound's healed. Why three days precisely? My friend, have you any idea why? It's quite simple, too.

Because time has exhausted itself! All of the psychic energy stolen from us by the silent madness of mortality is left over for us in the form of tremendous life-energy.

And all the rulers of the world will come to me to be operated on. Sorry, ladies and gentlemen, but the poor come first and so I have to take care of them—besides, their condition's more critical. Emperors will have to wait their turn, of course.

My discovery's rather elementary, isn't it, my dear colleague? Definitely worth having been thought of.

But until the hour for surgical intervention arrives, we are provided with a drug to be taken orally, and which is useful against time, temporarily: absinthe. Merely a symptomatic treatment. We won't be needing it much longer, since the surgical method's both radical and excellent. Cheers, my dear colleague!

Meeting Mother

My mother died giving me birth. The room stank of medicines and blood steamed here and there. People tip-toed whispering.

Morning was still far off. Very far. My pretty little mother, sighing a prayer in pain, held out for it desperately, vainly. She was dead when I took my first gasp. She sighed a long, hard sigh: she loved my father, and was only twenty.

And I forgot her. Never even asked about her. It never once struck me that I too had to have had a mother, that because of me she had gone to her grave early, moldering away, and that she was—actually—me.

So the years have passed.

I've seen lots of girls since then. They swept my pale yet fevered face with the fragrance of their hair, held my thin, bony waist in their soft, lazy, pink arms, shut my scorning lips with delectable kisses radiating the thrills of death. And yet never making me recall my mother, who died long ago, sighing long and hard, in a blood-spattered room stinking of medicaments.

Last night though she came to mind. Where from? But now I know I had to meet her.

I'd come back late from a woman and fallen asleep dazed and worn out. In a little while I made her out far off. She was coming closer. Young and fresh she was, as though just getting over giving birth.

I was trying to hide myself, but she caught sight of me and sank her dark blue eyes into mine.

A sadness mixed with joy shone gently in her small, pale face, and it compelled me to run to kiss and hug her. She was so lovely, so young. She didn't let me kiss her hand (which still surprises me).

She wore a clean cotton frock and a big, old-fashioned straw bonnet. I've seen the same dress, faded, stained, hanging in my grandmother's wardrobe. The stains were Grandma's tears, wept on late windy afternoons into my mother's old dress.

We reached for each other's arms, sensing the link that had been broken between us in that bleeding, medicine-reeking dawn—and we began again slowly, together.

It was Maytime around us. Far off over the fields was a harp strumming, a singing flute. Lilies-of-the-valley hummed sweet scents for us.

We stopped in that refuge of green field and blue sky. Our eyes met and tears flooded our faces. And we were smiling.

Ah, how young, how lovely my mother was! I picked the lilies-of-the-valley and strewed them over her, covering her girl's breasts—that had never suckled me—while she gazed at me with silent laughter, until my hands were empty of flowers.

Then we went on over the fields towards the blue wood. Hand in hand we paced, gazing up, happy to have each other.

But oh, suddenly, we reached the blue wood.

Violin and harp were fading in the distance. We both grew sad then. Holding each other, we roamed in the still, dewy meadows, watching the twilight mist coil about our legs.

We had to part at the edge of the wood. I wanted to hug my lovely dead mother yet one last time. She looked at me with an offended expression, but then stroked my face forgivingly.

Stepping lightly, she ran off into the wood. The evening breeze had come up and almost tore her hat away, but she caught it so gracefully. She turned to wave goodbye, standing for a long moment there, and then like a white wraith vanishing.

I stood there at the edge of the blue wood, my sight following after her sorrowing, adoring—long, long.

I think of her every day now. For her I've left the dark-haired women and the girls with their sweet voices—and dream now of my lovely twenty-year-old mother who died one dark morning.

Died sighing, long and hard.

Murder

I met the rich Zoltán Gerő's son, Béla, in the dining-car on the express.

—Where you headed? I said.

—Pest. For keeps. Can't stand home any more.

—Your father?

—Him, too. You know, the pay-scales... and so forth.

—Socialism wouldn't appeal to the old man, naturally.

—Nor my being a socialist, to say the least.

—Not quite the thing for the heir to an estate.

—This time I've got other reasons for clearing out though.

—Oh? Like what?

—You haven't heard about it?

—Nothing.

—Well, believe it or not, old pal, I've killed a man.

—Is that so?

—Killed him, all right. Sounds easy, huh? Well, it damn well was. Went like this...

Two weeks ago, 20th of July it was, I went to bed around midnight. Had a headache and couldn't get to sleep. Tossed and turned a good full hour. Then I heard a sort of grinding and sawing sound. Sheer accident—I'd been leaning my aching forehead on the wall, when I heard this peculiar rattling. I pulled back. Heard nothing. Pressed my ear to the wall again, and there it was. Rattle must have been coming from someone down at the end of the verandah. I listened for the dogs but they didn't bark, so I re-laxed again.

You know me, I'm nervous. That makes me yellow. That's another hangup I have with my dad. He thought I'd inherit his optimistic temperament and fearlessness, just as I'd get the coat-of-arms. But I'm a coward. Still, when I heard that sound again, I said to myself, I'll solve this mystery! Anyway I had no choice because the family sleeps in the building up front—and that's about three hundred yards from where I was, in the old manor down below.

It's an odd coincidence, but that very evening I'd been arguing with my father at dinner how silly, how illogical it was to punish theft so severely—after all, anybody with a stomach, and who hasn't got a stomach! has a natural right to eat. And if he's got nothing to eat, then he's got the right to steal. So as I say, we'd been discussing these problems....

...Anyway, I had my pants and socks on in a second. Holding my breath, I opened the door. Whether my head-ache was to blame or not, I don't know, but I wasn't in the least scared. I listened. The burglar was working stealthily, like an expert almost. I recall smiling to myself there in the dark at the word "expert." I felt my arms then. I seemed strong. One thing only I wanted: to see that thief, even for a second, just to see his face, his body. I was wondering if I could fight him. I can't explain it to you, but I felt so brave that I actually began enjoying the thrill.

I heard him raise the window, slit the drapes, and climb into the smoking-room, where the business things are kept in the safe. By that time I'd already sneaked into the library. Only one door between us now. I heard a match striking, and I was suddenly bathed in sweat. At that moment I realized just how insanely worked up I was. I was shaking like crazy, my heart pounding, my muscles all quivering, my mouth dry as a board. I lay down on my face to see if he had a light. Not a sliver came under the door—but I could hear him working on the safe.

That's it, he's standing at the safe! I crept right to the door. My heart was pounding in my throat, in my ears, my belly, and even in my toes. I was drunk on my own courage... and I threw the door open.

Two steps, and I'm at the safe and—just as I'd figured it—crashing into the burglar. A grunt from him—the fellow's paralyzed with terror. He clamped his teeth in my right arm, and I had to punch at his eyes with my left. That's how our scrimmage started, in utter darkness. All that panicky guy could do was bite me; but I pressed him to the floor and squeezed with my knees till his ribs cracked. He was gasping for air and spitting like a toad. When I held his head down, he bit into my sleeve. I took him by the throat with both hands, my fingers locked like steel clamps. I put all my strength into that steady, unrelenting pressure. I was getting heady from the effort and the sheer, bestial pleasure of killing.

He kept on scraping at my hands, weakly. Then his hands fell away and he moaned. Moaned three times, horribly. I wasn't counting, but I can hear those moans still coming, one after another. That body of his was completely in my power, but I couldn't—do you follow me?—just couldn't pull my hands from the throat. How long I was like that I can't say—maybe a minute, maybe three hours. But I recall very clearly my feeling of victory turning into a sense of being worn out, and nauseated.

My brains had evaporated and I would sit there on him in the dark like an imbecile wringing that wretched neck until the day of doom.

Suddenly I was aware that that neck was ice-cold stiff. I jumped off and ran to my room for a light. With my candle I came back for a look at him. It was last year's coachman, Peter, a narrow-chested, haggard, unshaven peasant with a straggling mustache.

He was staring at me with bulged, yellow eyes, his face purple. Dead. I was shocked, and getting scared. Impulsively, I tried to revive him: I rubbed him, I splashed his face with water. Then, pretty far gone myself, I went in circles for a while until it occurred to me what to do: call the servants. It was then I saw our three dogs sprawled dead in the courtyard. I set two of our fellows to doing artificial respiration on him and sent another for the doctor. We were still lifting and dropping Peter's arms by candlelight when he came back saying the doctor was out. We kept on trying to resuscitate him for another three hours till morning, but it was no use. Finally, I had to accept the fact that I'd killed a man, like it or not. Strangled a poor, weak, little peasant.

I looked round the room then. There was a slight grooving on the Wertheim safe—three inches long. Next to his poor body on the floor, Peter's burgling kit: a worn file, a hammer, a drill with a replacement handle fashioned crudely of pine, and a bent saw. Such were the tools he was using to crack a Wertheim safe! It would have taken him till the end of time.

You know, as I looked at those miserable tools like pitiful kid's toys strewn around Peter, and at his bulging eyeballs, an awful feeling of regret took me by the throat. I almost howled it out: poor Peter! What a shame that I should have assaulted with all my strength this weak man whose wretched life was ruined by hard work and poverty—sheer disgrace! Do you follow me? That was the worst thing about it all. And I couldn't undo it.

Béla Gerő seemed almost about to cry again with the recollection. I tried to say something to him, but it was no use. He'd gone silent. He paid no attention to me, but sat staring out the window of the express into the passing countryside.

Little Emma

I found this story in a diary. The boy who wrote it was a remote relation, and did away with himself at twenty. His mother recently died and the diary came into my hands. I had for a while no opportunity to examine it, but last week I began reading it, and was surprised by its casual, and simple, directness. I found some interesting items in the third notebook, and transcribe them here, offering them a little condensed, and with a few corrections in punctuation.

Little Emma was the prettiest of my kid sister Irma's friends. Her sweet little face with its gray eyes and her blonde hair seemed lovely to me from the first.

I was in my second year, she and Irma first graders. Other boys liked her too, but never said so because they were ashamed to admit noticing a girl and a first grader too.

But I knew right away I loved her and would always love her, and would marry her too one day, though I was ashamed of it.

Little Emma often came over to play with my two kid sisters and my brother Gábor. Sometimes there were other girls, like Ani and Juli, our nieces, whom we used to kiss in the cellar, in the attic, the garden and woodshed.

September was lovely and warm, and the balmy weather was even more enjoyable than summertime because I was back at school from two to four and eight to eleven in the morning, and playing ball outside was so much fun. We never tired: we'd run home for a snack, come right out and play till supper.

School was also more fun—more interesting. The new teacher, that is, Michael Sladek—tall with a red face and a thick voice—used a cane.

Our house was in the fifth district, and so our school was on the edge of town. Most of the boys were peasants. Some went barefoot and wore checked calico shirts; others had boots and velveteen trousers. I envied them because I felt them to be different, tougher and braver than I. There was one called Zöldi, four or five years older than anyone else: he carried a jackknife in the cuff of his boot. He showed it to me once, saying, even God can't scare me!

I told my brother, who didn't believe me.

Our new teacher didn't give us reading or let us do handwriting the way our nice first-grade teacher had. Instead he lectured at us, and then called us up to the blackboard to report. If someone talked or fooled around, he'd warn him just once; the next time, he called him up and said, slowly, Lie down, boy! And he'd turn to the class and say, He gets three. Who wants to give them?

This was exciting. Ten or fifteen boys usually stood. The teacher would review the volunteers, call one forward, and hand him the cane.

—If you don't give it to him as hard as you can, you're next!

The class would watch the beating and hear the howling in dead silence. We all admired the ones who didn't yell or weep; but I felt we hated them a bit, too. I've thought about this, but can't explain it.

As for me, punishment didn't scare me. I was perfectly aware that the teacher would think twice about it, my father being a Major and carrying a saber—he wouldn't have the guts to cane me.

The teacher found out soon enough that Zöldi was best at it, and from then on he did the punishing and did it well. His way of holding the cane differed from the others'. Hardly an hour passed without at least one or two "strokes." And then there were those warm, golden afternoons when we were all so restless—then, the whole of our second hour was taken up from three to four by canings. A boy huddled weeping in every other row.

One of those times I had a nosebleed and was allowed down to the janitor for water to wash it off. The bleeding stopped and I was going up again when I saw little Emma in the girls' corridor on the ground floor. She stood at her classroom door, her back to me, but she noticed me anyway. Obviously she was there being punished. I went to her, wanting to kiss her and sympathize, but she didn't seem at all unhappy. We said nothing, we only looked at each other. She was sweet and proud. As though she meant to make me realize my father was a mere Major, whereas hers was a Lieutenant-Colonel. She took her braid, untied its pink ribbon, and made a new bow. I watched her at my leisure. Each time she glanced up at me my heart beat.

She came to see us the next afternoon and asked me to keep it a secret—she'd been punished and had had to stand outside the door. I said nothing about it. But that evening I asked Irma why.

—None of your business, was her answer.

Disgusting Irma! I'd have loved hitting her right then, kicking her everywhere. She was jealous, she didn't want me loving Emma, and she didn't want Emma to love me.

She wouldn't let her play hide-and-seek with me, but stayed beside her, coddling and kissing and hugging her. She even stopped me from talking to Emma by calling her away, linking her arm in hers and strolling down at the far end of the yard. It made me bitter every time.

However, their close friendship soon turned to hatred. I noticed one day that they left school with different girls. Emma didn't come to visit after that. I asked my sister why they'd broken up, but she turned and ran off. For spite I told Father at table. Irma refused to answer his questions, so she had to go kneel in the corner, and she didn't get an apple either!

Weeks have passed. Uselessly I tried to talk my sister into making up with Emma, but she's stubborn and silent. Her eyes are misty with tears though, and she cries in bed for no reason.

Towards the middle of October, a terrible thing happened at school. For a change the teacher wanted Zöldi to be the first one caned. He called him, Come here nicely now!

Zöldi said nothing, but stood there.

The order came, Drag him here!

A dozen boys surrounded him, even some from the last rows. Many of us were scared of Zöldi, and sore at him too. Even I hated him and at first, no use lying, wanted to help drag him out. But it crossed my mind my father would be contemptuous of me if he ever heard I had ganged up with a crowd against one kid. So I stayed in my seat, choked up, my knees shaking. The boys were puffing and panting, trying to shove Zöldi out of his row; a few were grabbing at his legs where he held to the footboard; others were working to force his fingers from their fierce grip on the bench. It took them at least five minutes to budge him out

94

of there and get him down on the floor, where he pinned himself tight again. He didn't dare strike any of them though, because he must have realized that the teacher, who stood on a chair watching the scuffling, would have interfered. Sladek's face was brick-red with rage.

Finally they all latched on to Zöldi by his arms and legs. They dragged him up to the desk, scraping his back along the floor.

—Don't let him get away! the teacher shouted. Turn him on his face and hold his hands and feet down good!

With all their strength, exhilarant, the boys followed his orders. Zöldi could get hold of nothing, and they kneeled on his arms, four squatting on his legs, two of them leaning on his head. This was the moment the teacher was waiting for. Calmly he crouched beside them, disposed the boys so none of them would be in the way of the cane, and went to work then, dealing Zöldi half a dozen strokes. They sounded awful. Thick, sharp whistles. I burst into a chilled sweating, yet as if held in a magnetic field, stood on my toes on the footboard so as to miss nothing of the sight. The teacher stopped. Zöldi has taken them all without a peep.

—Will you stop being so *stubborn*, Sladek said quietly. And after waiting, dizzy with rage, he hollered: Answer!

But Zöldi didn't answer.

—All right, my boy, the teacher hissed, it makes no difference to me if you don't answer now—because you will later!

And furiously, faster and faster he went on with the caning. I couldn't even count the blows anymore. Despite all the strength in that big man, he was panting with exhaustion. Finally he stopped, worn out, and hoarsely demanded again, Will you *stop* being so *stubborn!*

Still no response from Zöldi.

The teacher mopped his brow and went on with his "strokings," slower now, pausing after each one and repeating, *Will you stop being so stubborn!*

This went on for another dozen "strokings." Then a terrible howl: Nooo!

The teacher laid the cane down and sent the boys to their seats. Zöldi got to his feet, fixing up his ripped clothes as best as he could—they had been torn in the scuffling—and returned to his place. His face was smudged from the floor, tears fell on his jacket, and he spat blood.

The teacher, however, called him back.

—Who said you could sit down! Get back here right away!

Zöldi staggered up front again, his head hanging. Sladek rubbed his palms together as though he'd just finished a neat bit of work, and said gently, with an unctuous, charitable voice, My dear fellow, you must realize I gave you that as a warning for the next time. It's most ungrateful in you to disobey your teacher. I discern in you an unfortunate tendency, so I think I shall have to slap your face too.

The slap, however, became a few slaps, and he went on and on slapping Zöldi's face until the boy sank dazed against the blackboard. But he pulled himself away and ran out the door. The teacher cursed and slammed it after him, and then seated himself at his desk again. You could have heard a pin drop.

I got home, ran a temperature, and became delirious. I was put to bed. My father came and questioned me in the evening. I had to tell him what had gone on at school.

My parents execrated Sladek, and the next week I went to another school in the best part of town.

I couldn't see Emma every day then. My heart bled.

I read in the paper of October 25th that some coachman had been hanged for robbing and killing one of his fares. A long description of his behavior on death row and in the morning under the gallows. That night my parents discussed it at dinner, and my father described a hanging he'd witnessed when he was twenty.

—How I'd like to have seen it, I cried.

—Be grateful you haven't, he said. And don't you ever go to one, because you'll dream about it for seven years as I did.

After school next day, I suggested to my brother Gábor that we might build ourselves a gallows, and string up a dog or cat. Gábor liked the plan, and we worked on one in the attic. We stole a clothesline and made a noose. We quit work on the gallows because we hadn't a handy beam for it, and also worried that our parents would stop us if we arranged hangings out in the yard.

Gábor wasn't too keen on torturing animals, though once he got started he came up with great ideas. The year before, for instance, he'd sliced a cat alive with the carving knife. That was in the garden. Ani and Juli trapped the cat, all of us held him down on his back, and Gábor slashed him down his belly.

We got the rope up over a rafter in the attic. A dachshund had strayed in from the road that afternoon, and we shut the gate, caught him, and lugged him up. The girls were jubilant as Gábor and I calmly prepared.

—You're Judge, Gábor pronounced, and I'm the

Hangman. And I'm reporting: Your Honor, everything's in readiness for the execution!

—Excellent, I said. Hangman, you may do your job!

And I lifted the dog as Gábor tugged at the rope. Then when he commanded, I suddenly let go. The dachshund whimpered distressfully, kicking his yellow-spotted black feet. But he soon went limp and still. We looked at him awhile and then went for our snack, leaving him dangling there. Afterwards the girls hung around the gate and lured another dog in with a lump of sugar. Lugging it in their skirts, they brought it to Gábor for another execution, but he refused, saying one hanging a day was enough. Juli opened the gate and let him out.

For a few days we forgot all about it because we had a new ball and Gábor and I played catch steadily.

Later on we were talking about Emma. Gábor said he hated her because she was a showoff; he said Irma was stupid for having been so crazy about her.

—I hope they never make up; otherwise she'll be back here boasting and all, Gábor said angrily.

Gábor didn't get his wish, because the very next afternoon Irma brought Emma in with her.

—She's repulsive, Gábor whispered to me.

—She's a sweet darling, I said to myself, though I was sore at Irma, too. Because Irma was flooded with pleasure and while we were playing kept calling her aside to hug her and practically choke her with kisses. Yet they quarrelled later anyhow.

—So you won't promise not to talk to Rosie anymore? Irma said, almost in tears.

—I certainly shan't, Emma said firmly, with a grin.

Juli and Ani whispered to one another. Irma, Gábor, and

I were all looking at little Emma—God, how beautiful she was!

Those sunny autumn afternoons were growing to a close. The yard was ours alone: Father and Mother went riding, the cook gave us our cocoa and went back to work in the kitchen.

—Have you ever seen a hanging? my sister asked Emma afterward.

— No! said Emma, with a shake of the head, her hair brushing her cheeks.

— But you've heard about it from your father, haven't you?

—Yes. He said a murderer was hanged, she replied coldly, uninterested.

—You know something? We've got a scaffold all our own, Juli declared.

And we got Emma up in our attic to see an execution. Gábor and I had buried the dachshund in a dump a few days earlier. The noose dangled there emptily.

—Now we can play hanging, Irma said. Emma must be convicted, and we must hang her.

—We should do it to *you*, Emma laughed.

—Hangman, do your job, said Gábor, giving himself the order.

Little Emma paled, but still smiled.

—Don't move! Irma said.

And I looped the noose about Emma's neck.

—Not me, I don't want to be hanged, the little girl whimpered.

—The murderer begs our mercy, Gábor intoned flushing, but the Hangman's assistants seize the condemned! Ani and Juli took her arms.

—No, I won't let you! little Emma screamed, and started crying.

—Mercy is with the Most High, Gábor recited. And Irma lifted her friend up by her thighs.

She couldn't manage it and staggered. I went to her and helped. It was the first chance I'd ever had to hold Emma in my arms. My brother yanked at the line, wrapped his end around the rafter and tied it. Little Emma swung there. At first, she flailed her arms about, and kicked her short, thin, white-stockinged legs. Her movements seemed very odd. I couldn't see her face because the attic was quite dark by then. Suddenly the movements ceased. Her body stretched, as though it were seeking something to stand on. And then she moved no more. A ghastly fright took us all. We dashed recklessly down from the attic, scattering and hiding in the garden. Ani and Juli ran home fast.

Half an hour later, the cook, fetching something from up there in the attic, found her body. She called Emma's father over, before our parents had even come home....

The notes recording this incident stop there. The diary's author, whose misfortune it had been to have become a participant in this terrible thing, never mentions it again. All I know about the later history of the family is that the father retired as a Colonel, Irma is a widow today, and Gábor an officer in the Army.

Opium

...from a neurologist's mail

For Attila Sassy

True, waking up mornings brings lingering suffering. Unbearable suffering. The morning light roars through the street in thundering chords. Neither frosted glass nor dark drapery can protect one from it, its insulting rhythms penetrating everything, calling one away to mean, inferior beings who believe that merciless vile music the Law of Life and what they live, Life.

Alert, they leap from beds in which they slept through stuporous dreamlessness. They scrub themselves, praising the cold water, though it pains them. They go to work with brawn and brain, and their fatigue shames this heart that no longer needs miserable pleasantries but the one thing merely: the doleful pleasure which says, We have escaped the fray, victorious; we may rest in bloody exhaustion. No pleasure, that: merely cessation of pain. Insensitive to pain, bearing it patiently seems enough to them, and more than enough. They are the wicked. Nonetheless, one shouldn't be angered by them, even if it's their fault that Life cannot be arranged solely for the sake of ancient and holy pleasure—which is, of course, living's whole purpose.

True, one pays for it: the light returning each morning takes its ruthless toll. Wearied heartbeat; eyelids scarcely supporting the sunlight's weight; a skin fearful of the wind. Muscles displeased and reluctant to do their work. The body shudders from the shock of raucous voices, and pain

lies hidden, coiled about the base of the skull. So one can't laugh at those morons' petty doings, accomplished with such pother and shouting and fatigue. Actually, what makes escape from worry, sharp noises, and the boring monotonousness of life's bullying rhythms impossible, is the light. And one can communicate by means of words only, which has nothing to do with the concepts in one's brain, strictly speaking.

More things show up like this to make their reports in the sun's withering rays.

Our face in the mirror reflects mere shapeless, stiff blotchings that have nothing to do with us, obviously. Trains pull into stations and people and horse-drawn carriages trot past in the streets. How marvelous all that is, and conducive to suffering; at the same time strange, incomprehensible, leading to the conviction that in their present forms things have neither reason nor purpose. Hence one must escape somewhere—where problems are simpler and more easily resolved.

Pleasure erases contours, dissolves senselessness, freeing us from the shackles of space, halting the rattling of the clock's seconds: it lifts us on its sultry undulations to the highest reaches of Life.

There to remain, if but for moments, trembling and fearful of coming down—misery indeed. Yet most people count themselves rewarded with the pittance of those few moments. What else is there for them? They haven't the strength or the courage to risk themselves in a splendid, enduring pleasure that rocks them to eternity. This risk is cheap, absurdly small. True, ten hammering hours of malicious, murderous daylight go tediously by; but for those fourteen evening and night hours we experience a portion of eternity's mystery and timeless wonder.

In that time we recognize life's deepest meaning; the opacity, the darkness is made bright. Like the lips of fresh and gentle girls, sound like kisses showers our bodies. In our spine, in our skull, color and line buzz new yet ancient and clear. And now, *no longer resembling* the color and line to which we are accustomed, they reveal the grand secrets hidden in forms. That primitive and so very flawed knowledge of Life we had gained through sight, hearing, smell, taste and touch is now improved, and made whole. We are given the chance to learn the truth of Life inherent in each of us, all of truth, perfected, beyond the faculties of our senses. A truth inexpressible in words or by concepts and judgments, just as the senses cannot recognize it. What right have I to say I know the weight of a cube, when I have merely seen but never lifted it? The same is true of one who has only seen, heard, smelled, tasted, touched: he has no right to say he's lived. Pleasure alone can give us knowledge of things and God's joy. Yet may we say that God's joy endures for a moment only? Yes, for that is what He doles out to fools and cowards. But those who, desirous of more, deserve more, they have a chance to steal from eternity—through noble, heroic daring.

They must forego the capacity to see and hear well. Opium, horrible and blessed connection of pleasure, destroys our organs and senses. The healthy appetite and the bourgeois sensation of feeling good and tired have to be sacrificed. The eyes water, the ears ring. Objects, printed words, people look faded. Sounds and words wander randomly in the tiny mechanisms of the organs of hearing.

Stop those miserable, inferior little contraptions!

In some quiet little room where sounds die on thick carpeting and stained glass scatters the lamp's low flickering flame—lie down there on your back. Shut your eyes. And the tiny opium pipe will lead you to where we live for the sake of Life alone and nothing more. That is after all the only be-all and end-all. And even our miserly God gave each one of his pitiable worms a few seconds of life, just to live to go on living to procreate. And the new worm gets his share of a second, too.

So costly an item is the essence of Life that whole generations and centuries can be given but a single hour of it.

Whoever agrees to this also agrees to die before he's ever even been born. However, those who can grow to be men, who have taken things into account as befits their pride, should seize fourteen hours of it a day, every day. Those fourteen hours are equivalent to eight thousand years in the lives of four hundred generations. But let's call it only five thousand. Hence in one single day I live five thousand years. In one single year I live about two million years. Suppose you pick up on opium as a strong, well-developed adult and take good care of your health—best left to a skilled doctor—why, then you can live for ten years. And then at twenty million years of age you can let your head fall on the icy pillow of eternal annihilation.

As for those who don't wish to pay the price, who don't desire twenty million years of life eternal—let them live a hundred years increasing and multiplying.

A Young Lady

To Professor Moravcsik

I

I got a letter one day from Philip. He asked me—in the jumbled chaos of the paralytic's hand—to visit him as soon as I could.

Usually, I saw him every other week. I used to go more often a year and a half ago, when he had first been admitted to the sanatorium. Recently, however, I'd been running into his wife there—quite a blooming beauty—and noticed poor Philip's jealousy as we said goodbye to him and walked out together; so I went only now and then, making sure his wife wasn't with him.

He really had no reason to be jealous. I only escorted this beauty home and left her at her gate.

Philip loved his wife very much. He married late, at thirty-five, and like many another pale, greedy neurotic, took a tall, handsomely endowed girl with an ivory skin, blonde hair and blue eyes. A sweet-smelling blonde girl on whose red, full lips sensuality was blooming. Philip was madly in love, broke with his friends, stopped going out, and spent every free hour with his wife. I hated him a little for it, but also pitied him a little.

When he was paralyzed, my pity for him grew, my hatred vanished.

His situation was altogether miserable.

Once on a spring afternoon that was full of dazzling sunshine, he made love to his wife in my presence. He wanted her to desire him.

Stammering, blushing, and vexed by the hopeless stumblings of his tongue, he was calling her a darling and a sweetheart and the most beautiful woman in the world—and signaling to me to leave the room. Meanwhile she glanced at me, scared, begging not to be left alone with that sick man. This healthy, trim woman was trembling with fear. I could have forgiven her for it, but I came to feel that her fright was rooted in a heartless, nasty selfishness. She must never have truly loved him, if she couldn't bravely endure his kisses now.

I realized that clearly just then, and left the room so she'd know my feelings about it. I found out later that she had rung for the nurse as soon as I'd gone away.

Philip hasn't mentioned his wife since. He didn't care about her, no longer looked at her, and never asked her to give him her hand to hold. He also stopped showing any interest in his pretty nurse, though he'd formerly drawn my attention to her evident assets.

2

One afternoon I went to visit him.

I noticed a singular change in him. His features, once handsome, open and manly, were now childlike, smoothed, filled with the adoring joyfulness of some unknown rapture. His expression was solemn though pleasant.

—My friend, I-I am very ha-happy… you ca-came. I want to tell you something… He smiled happily enough, and held my hands.

My friend, he said, for the last week I've been noticing that I've got someone special here… a pretty, young lady.

He pronounced that last phrase as though he were praying, as though he were a child trying to tell his brother

108

or sister a story he'd heard, trying to convey all that was touching, lovely, and full of wonder in his heart, and tell it all, without losing a word of it.—A young lady, he said.

—What young lady? I said.

—A beautiful, a lovely young lady. She takes care of me and spends every minute with me. She talks to me—she's bringing back my health.

—What does she tell you? I asked, curious.

—Lots of things, she's talking to me now.

—About what?

Philip looked up, attentive, at the round face of the clock on the wall opposite him, and smiled.

—That you're really a good friend to me.

—The clock says so, or the young lady?

—The young lady. She speaks with the voice of the clock. It's her voice I hear coming from it. She talks about everything clearly and distinctly with the clock's ticking.

—And what else has she told you?

—That I'll recover completely. Only I have to be patient.

—Of course! I said, dismayed by the reproach implied by the young lady's words. It struck me that neither Philip's wife nor I had promised him he'd recover. We'd just assumed he was resigned to being incurable.

—And how long has this young lady been watching over you?

—Constantly. Ever since I came. She says she's been taking care of me from the day I was brought here. She remembers it all. Philip smiled again, was quiet a bit, and resumed, Isn't that nice? She just said that I was crying in my bed on the first night I was brought, and wasn't that childlike of me!

—What's her voice like?

—Her voi-voice, my friend, is a sweet one.... Once when I was a third grader, a woman substituted for our teacher. A young woman, brown-haired, in a white dress—and she had the very same voice, soft, pleasant, like music. I could listen to it all day. And what is so nice is that she talks to me as soon as I ask her to.

He grew quiet, waiting as though his thin ears were alive. He looked like a mummy on his white pillow, lying there unmoving, his head alone showing—like an infant's head out of its swaddling. Then he said that the young lady had comforted him, and told him that one of his favorite dishes would be served tonight, farina in milk.

—Did you tell your wife about the young woman? I asked.

—Oh no, he said somberly, avoiding the question without a hint of embarrassment. Nobody knows but the head surgeon and you. I didn't even tell his assistant about her, because he talks to my wife downstairs and would tell her. She wouldn't like it. And I ask you not to mention that to her either.

—No, no, absolutely not, I said, it would only upset her and make her jealous.

A lull in our conversation. Then Philip went on, I could tell you, oh, so much about her.... She's the kind of woman I always wanted, but never came across.

—Will you marry her when you're better?

My question didn't shock him. He thought about it a little, and said, No, why should I marry her? I'd have a hard time getting a divorce. She said herself I mustn't divorce my wife. I mustn't hurt anyone, she said, and she'd be with me always, like now. She loves me truly and selflessly.

A fly landed on Philip's face. The patient smiled, and didn't shake it off.

—See that fly on my forehead? he said, grinning. She sent it to me, too. The flies are buzzing, making music, singing her messages in my ear. She always sends me good news.

—And what did this fly just tell you?

—This... this one... wait.... Nothing. But she sent it anyway. These flies don't bite, these flies don't bother me. He took some crumbs out of his handkerchief and pasted them on his balding head. This is for the flies, he whispered, smiling. I feed the flies. And look at the floor. You won't believe it, but it's filled with electricity. The doctor himself knows nothing about it. She sends it too, to heal me. And I am healing: the current surges up through the legs of the bed and circulates in me constantly. I am stronger every day. It affects me quite differently from that electrical treatment the assistant gives me in the morning. I'd be dead by now with that one—only hers cures me by the minute.

—What's her name, I interrupted Philip.

—Her name... her name? I don't know. She never told me, though I've asked her many times. Philip waited, watching the clock, and then smiled. She just said I mustn't ask her, I should be satisfied that she loves me. My friend, till now I never knew about a love like this. I feel it constantly, and I'm happy. Look at the roof there—see those lovely birds on the wires? She's the one who sends them, too. When I'm bored, I watch them flying and pursuing each other. They amuse me. And they carry messages from her, too.

I looked out. The birds were just common crows.

—What color are they? I can't make it out, I said.

—Brilliant: blue and green. Some of them even have golden feathers.

—All right, I said, in other words, you're a happy man, Philip. You're in good hands, and you've got everything going for you.

3

I said goodbye. Going down, I met the assistant.

—It's amazing, he said. This newly-acquired obsession of his, supported by delusion and hallucination. It's a perfect illustration and shows that, apart from any other symptoms, and no progressive debility, the psyche guards itself from the unpleasant, terrible and ultimately unbearable impressions the body it's attached to would reveal in moments of clarity. It doesn't often happen that easily. Some patients weep for days on end, and one realizes that they are clearly aware of their condition and their fate; but then their rescue theory sort of automatically shows up in a set of delusions. In a few days' time, the patient turns himself into a king, an emperor, Napoleon, into a magnate or an athlete, and clings tenaciously to that one saving idea that makes it possible to go on living. Our patient has created an ideal for himself in the form of a girl whose voice he hears in the clock's ticking: she tells him all sorts of pleasant, beautiful things, and most of all she tells him he's recovering. There is not a hint of sexuality in her relation to him.

—Yes, I know, I said. I was a little annoyed by the conceit in his voice, the pompous phrasing of the young man in white, and I left quickly.

So, I thought, elaborating the idea in my head, not only

I and the head surgeon know Philip's secret, but the assistant does too, told by his chief. The assistant will in turn tell Philip's wife his secret. And Philip's wife won't hesitate a moment longer—as she has until now—to cheat on Philip with the assistant.

And she'll be right—I drew my conclusion unpityingly.

Festal Slaughter

The long winter's night was ending. There was a strip of gray below the sky, there were the fields halted in a line of mist, far beyond the cluster of dark houses. Overhead stars still sparkled. Down here, in the shadowless dark depth of houses where sleeping folk lay breathing, that strip of gray was as yet unperceived.

Rosie turned in bed, opened her eyes, and glanced out. Without thinking she slipped out and pattered over the cold bricks of the kitchen, unaware of the icy floor. Ruffling her hair from her face and striking a light, she waited for the match to burn high, lit the kitchen lamp with it, and set to work. No need for her to dress—she slept in her clothes, only removing her bodice at night. She combed her hair, rapidly braiding and putting it up with two pins. (Her fine hair was straw-blonde and not much bother to her.) She wet her ruddy, fifteen-year-old's face, rubbed it, and soaped her strong, chapped hands, the backs of which were covered with yellow down.

She was mechanical and quick about it. Fishing out her clogs, she made her bed and left the kitchen.

There was frost outdoors, the stones in the yard were slick, and the girl slipped. Jesus Christ! she cried through clenched teeth.

At the far end of the yard the sow was rooting and grunting. She was to be slaughtered today. Rosie went to pat her.

—So, my dearie, you're up, too, poor thing. Tough on

you, but today we're going to kill you, poor thing. He'll come with his big knife and slit your gizzard, you poor soul, you.

The sow grunted and nuzzled her. The girl left her and scuffled down to the cellar where she lit a fire under the great kettle.

The biting January cold seemed to have crept down here, too, and wrapped itself into the floor and walls. Rosie's strong, handsome body didn't shiver though, even in its thin clothes. She knelt on the icy stone, piled straw, then wood on the flames, and blew them up till they blazed and roared. Then she woke the cook, laid out the sharpened knives, and returned to the fire. The sow grunted at her through the cellar door, and Rosie answered. Doesn't matter what you think, dearie, you'll be killed today. The butcher's coming with his great big knife, and he'll shove it into your throat no matter how much you cry...!

The yard had turned gray while she'd been making up the fire; only a few stars were left in the sky. A man entered the yard. The butcher. A brawny peasant: grand mustaches, pockmarked cheeks—no way of saying whether he was twenty-five or forty. He went to the kitchen.

—Morning!

—Morning to you, too!

He laid his knives out quietly, removed his coat, rolled his shirtsleeves up, and tied an apron on. He was deliberate and neat in his motions, never taking his eyes from the girl. He poked the fire, dipped a finger into the water warming over it.

—Good girl, he said, patting her shoulder. Rosie didn't look up; she shook him off with exaggerated annoyance, and piled more straw on.

Everyone in the house was up soon and in the courtyard, the young gentlemen, the governess and children.

The sow was hustled in. The butcher walked up to her casually, gripped her head in his knees, held her down, and finished her off just like that. Rosie buried her face in her apron. The children were shouting, Rosie is a scaredy! Rosie is a scaredy!

The sow scarcely had a chance to groan. In sixty minutes' time she lay in the kitchen cut up into pieces of all sizes. The whole house reeked pork. Various cuts of meat, bacon and ham were spread on the kitchen table, pots were brimming with it, water boiling. The butcher, cook and Rosie worked hard and by noon only the sausages were left to do. The butcher, eating his dinner at the table and quaffing a few too many, was also mincing meat for the stuffing. The girls were emptying and scrubbing the guts. When they were done, Rosie showed them to the butcher.

—Not clean enough, he said. Don't spare those hands of yours, sweetie, he tickled her, because nothing gets done that way.

—Who the hell's sparing them, she retorted. Not me! and punched him in the back. And blushed.

Everything was done by late afternoon: sausage-rings, bacon, ham—all resting in the pantry. The butcher was still downstairs, cleaning away the bristles.

—Hey, Rosie, come over here!

No one in the cellar, the cook upstairs preparing supper. The fun part of pig-slaughtering was finished; the fatigue was left after hard work, a lassitude that insinuated itself through their heads with the heavy odors of blood and raw flesh. Outside, the winter night, cold; in the kitchen, the fire glowing warmly.

117

The butcher took Rosie by her waist as she came in, and his whole body pressed her hard.

Others had hugged her, but she'd never really felt them. She would wriggle away, hand out a thwack, and dash off. But now the strong arms held her, the sinewy ropes caught her, crushed her breath out. She was voiceless.

A little later she was pacing the yard, her face covered by her kerchief.

—Oh god, but I'd get it from Mamma if she knew. She'd just kill me, and serve me right, too. Poor Mamma warned me all right—if I was stupid I'd end up just like Juli Kovaks, just like Juli....

They called her in to make up the beds and serve at supper. There was a lot of work for her yet—even lulling the youngest one to sleep was her job. She played on the bed with the child, kissing it and rolling it around.

When at last she lay in her own bed, the thought of children passed through her head; she'd been reminded of it by the little one she'd just put to sleep.

—And I'll have one myself.... It's awful. She soothed herself, but couldn't help crying.

Her tears dried soon enough—Rosie was asleep, breathing deeply, evenly, as tired people do.

A Joseph in Egypt

Jóska Zalai—that clever, cheerful young man—stopped me in the street.

—I had such a marvelous, incredibly beautiful dream last night! I must tell you about it.

We went to a café, sat down, and lit up. I said I was all ears, and Joseph began.

—It was a summer morning. A fresh, lovely morning that hardly ever dawns in the life of nervous people. The rays of the sun poured joy into the air as thick as the paint in Naturalist canvases fifteen years ago. A placid region stretching out flat everywhere; palm trees; a pyramid far off. I must be in Egypt, and walking on the shores of that wide river, the Nile. I still had to find what period I was in. I thought about that as I strolled along the shore. Not a soul in sight. A few ibises patiently standing in the water.

Oh, sacred birds! I whispered in awe, and went on. At one spot, wading up to my ankles in the tepid wavelets, I glimpsed something brick red under me. I stopped to look at it closely: it was my own body reflected—can you visualize this?—my whole body was brick red. I had a white sash like an apron round my loins, and I was wearing some headgear like a pleated, lemon-colored kerchief hanging in folds behind my ears down to my shoulders, like a curtain. Ever since high school I've wondered how the Egyptians figured out that kerchief-folding, and it occurred to me here was the chance to find out. But I didn't take it off, because I was afraid that if I couldn't fix it up again I'd have to go bareheaded and bald in the hot sun. For my head was shaved smooth under the scarf. I decided to put the question off until I met an Egyptian with the same headgear, who'd teach me the kerchief-folding trick.

By now I'd a good suspicion that all this was happening three or four thousand years before Christ, but how I came to it I didn't for the life of me know.

I went on along the river bank, feeling younger and happier than I'd ever been. You couldn't begin to imagine such sheer happiness in real life, because when you're awake there's no real freedom. I was independent. In real life independence is both good and bad at once. Independence means father's not running things any more, but his love's waning, too. The kind that's altogether good and never a drop of the bad... it's only when you're dreaming. And now, as an Egyptian in a dream on the shore of the Nile, I belonged to no one. Yet my solitude disturbed me not at all. Alone and lonely though I was, my loneliness was unshadowed, untouched by pain.

And so there I was, in that moist, fresh light, strolling along through mild airs. My strange, sacred happiness was different from earthly delights because it had no insufferable aspects, as for instance viewing a landscape with deep, perfect joy is always unbearable.

You sigh, you disengage yourself from the magic. Why? Because if you don't, the joy imparted by it slowly fades; you tire of gazing, of feeling the music die; and that's even more distressing. Walking beside the Nile though, I'd altogether escaped this human misery, caused so obviously by our metabolism, which derives from basic organic laws. The joyousness of life sang inside me; an indelible melody, it

sang in the air about me, quiet, full, in a continuing beauty that renewed, refreshed me.

I ran, for miles and miles it seemed I ran, untiringly. My heart beat no harder, and my legs were no more tired than as if I were walking. I couldn't even hear myself breathing. The water sang lapping with a silvery tinkle at my feet. I would take small paces at times, and then again leapt swinging and whirling with rhythmical gorgeous arabesques. I suddenly realized that motion, any sort of movement at all, is one of those magnificent pleasures in life that goes unrecognized by us.

The point is, man oughtn't to be hindered by clothing. It's our clothing that impedes not merely our movement, but denies our skin the revelation of the resisting air—this unseen, wonderful atmosphere whose gas obediently yields to us, and then lightly breezes back into the space we've just vacated.

Occasionally I'd halt and look at the flora. Huge, white lotuses bloomed opulent and regal on the water, and the glittering green water plants around them made the perfumed white lotus petals pant dazzlingly. And the Nile rolled vast and slow. Though I walked so deliberately, I easily kept up with the current. On the far shore an endless blue line of palm groves, with narrow openings every so often through which the hazy distance of deserts glimmered. Looking back up the road I'd come to see if there were a boat or raft on the river, I saw something—a tiny, dark line swimming on the horizon's edge, and on it a dot of white.

It'll be sundown, I thought, by the time they reach me on the lazy Nile. Why should I wait for them? I said to myself,

I can find my way wherever I want, I've nothing urgent, no plans to go anywhere.

I waded in to my neck and went on my way swimming. I would take long strokes, and then float on my back on the waves, watching the cerulean sky with its light, long clouds fluttering over the river like the unseen rufflings of a gauzy, heavenly curtain. An ibis now and then climbed up over the shore, flapping slow wings until its slim, lovely body glided up through their undulations, vanishing in their invisible layers. This gave me incomparable, sublime delight, while the waters carried me slowly on and on.

Well, I said to myself, happiness can be quite simple. I'm happy because I've no desire to go anywhere. And I'd be perfectly content to know that I might swim the Nile on my back like this beneath the blue sky of the morning sun until the day I die.

However, that thought wasn't in the dream like that. I'm only putting it like that to you now in real-life language. Actually, my musing utterly lacked any profane comparison between life's values and death. In my dream, death didn't seem the worst of all possible evils, and life wasn't the best of all possible things. Everything seemed equally beautiful and good, wonderful and new all at once: and not in the least tiring or frightening as it is here in this vale of tears.

Meanwhile, I had been carried far from shore and was nearly in the middle when I suddenly glimpsed a woman on the bank. Her head was coifed in white cloth, and she knelt, washing clothes.

A human being at last, I said, though I wasn't overjoyed about it: "at last" didn't mean I'd wished to see a human being, nor expected to. I stood and watched, exposed from my shoulders up. The woman took no notice of me, but went on scrubbing. Lively, cheerful, she turned and rinsed and pounded the clothes.

Slowly I approached, and saw a yellow wooden dwelling between the trees not far from the water.

Probably the owner, I thought. So graceful was she, she couldn't have been a servant. A maid will wash in a more practiced manner, mechanically, without such charm, or so I reasoned.

Here's a woman who, though knowing herself unwatched, still works gracefully and with joy. A common soul would lack the noble capacity to delight in her own strong skill and beauty, which this woman showed by the way she worked.

I was intensely fascinated by her bronze, rounded shoulders, her black hair straying out in curls from beneath her headcloth, her opulent breasts restrained by a yellow band, her naked, shapely arms and her wide hips, so very delightful in that crouching posture. Yet my longing for her had none of that burning, depressing flavor that always comes with situations like that—which comes from the anxiety that she can't and won't be ours, or if she will, then not now. I stood in the water peacefully, not blinded by that fiery, sensual need, but enjoying the delightful scene undistracted.

She rose and slowly stretched. I could now admire the marvelous, unique proportions of her body: soft yet solid, and proportioned so well. She was tall, yet so graceful I believe I could easily have carried her. She put the garments in a basket and went towards the house. It seemed to me she hadn't seen me, and I was going to call out when she turned round abruptly with a friendly smile. I lifted my right arm to greet her and waded quickly towards shore. She stood looking gravely at me now, unmoving. I was soon before her. I bowed deeply, respectfully.

—Who are you, my dear woman?

—You must be able to see who I am by looking at me: I'm a Jewess. My husband's a student of the Law, and he's away just now.

—Would you permit me to rest at your house? A long journey has tired me.

—You must be hungry then. Would you like to eat?

—I'm not thinking of that now. Please don't be concerned to offer me food.

—If I offered bread, you wouldn't refuse me.

—What touches your hands is dear to me.

—Come into the house then.

The woman walked on ahead, and I could see how she tried to hold in that glorious undulation of her hips. Her little feet and slim ankles looked even more angelically lovely. At the door, she drew a light green cotton curtain aside for me.

—Enter, her voice sang.

I was in a small room whose walls were hung with white cotton drapes. There was a floor of matting. In the corner, a low table of woven cane, benches near it along both walls.

—This is where we live, she said, far from the city. My husband's protective and doesn't want me to lay eyes on other men.

—He's afraid you'll betray him?

—No, not that. Everyone knows the adulteress is stoned to death. But he doesn't want another man to rouse desire in me.

—Is your husband gone all day?

—He leaves in the morning for the house where they

gather to study the words of wisdom. In the evening he returns.

—Aren't you lonely?

—No, I work.

—Do you have children?

—No. But a holy man from Asia prophesied that I shall have them, and so I wait in patience. Now tell me about yourself. You're obviously an Egyptian from the Upper Nile. Is that where you live?

—Yes, I said, automatically.

—You're young. I can see—and I'm certain of it—luck will be with you.

—You sweet woman, what makes you think so?

—Because you look clever, and you have a very nice face.

She slipped from the room for a minute, then returned and set some bread in a yellow, earthen dish, and a red stoneware jug before me. Running her hands down her hips then, she sat opposite me.

—Aren't you afraid your husband may come back? I asked.

—No, he never returns home this time of the day, she answered casually.

I ate, and she watched me benevolently, her hands folded quietly in her lap. I looked closely at her lovely face now: she seemed between twenty-five and thirty. Her features were given a kind and sensual cast by the large, boldly-shaped nose with its finely-drawn nostrils. Her eyebrows were thin and high-arched. Intelligent, warm brown eyes; their dreamy lids covering a third of their dark brown and glowing irises. The gorgeous blue rings beneath her eyes suggested rich years of womanly knowledge and life's pleasures. Her full lips were moist and crimson. The evenly-bronzed skin, shading on her face towards the lightness of ivory, appeared velvety cool.

I said, and said it sincerely, What a fine, lovely woman you are.

—Oh no, she laughed. I'm already old. I was over eighteen when I wed, and it's ten years I've been a wife.

—So you're twenty-eight.

—Yes, twenty-eight.

We grew silent. Desire dried my throat. I swallowed a mouthful from the jug, and got up.

—Thank you for your hospitality, I said, holding her small hands.

—You're welcome, she replied, and rose too.

I looked at her lovely eyes which were moist, smiling, and at her features which revealed a tense, almost frightened severity. Then I kissed her lips and closed eyes, her beautiful soft arms, her full, ivory throat, the locks of hair that slipped out from her white kerchief, breathing the fragrance of cedar.

Feebly, tenderly, the woman's eyes closed beneath my kisses, her shoulders trembled, and she pressed her eyes shut as though trying to avoid the unbearable, overpowering shock of desire as one seeks to escape a sudden powerful light. Then she embraced me slowly and, holding me tight against her splendid loins, began kissing me sensually, avidly. Her brilliant eyes held mine hypnotically; they closed; they changed color, increasing my mad desire.... Oh, how miraculous!

—And now, please go, she said, stroking my face.

—Let me stay a while longer.

—You must leave now—do you want me to die? Do you

want me stoned to death, do you want my husband to live out his life in sorrow and shame? I want to live so that I may remember you and this happiness I have now had, something I'd never expected or even hoped to receive from God.

—May you be blessed a thousand times over, I said, my eyes full of tears. I kissed her little hands.

—May good fortune and happiness come to you in turn, she whispered in a warm, choked voice, kissing my shoulders.

I knelt before her, embracing her blessed hips, pressing kisses on her knees.

I left the house then, my heart full, aching. And yet I was happy. I held my arms out to the setting sun, and went out against the current. A stone's throw off, I turned.

The woman stood on the shore. With one arm she covered her eyes, reaching out towards me with the other. Her little fingers drooped like the wings of a wounded bird, and the magnificent lines of her form flared out again in the sun's golden sheen.

That's the last image I recall of my dream, said Jóska after a long silence. I've been thinking about that dream all day. The Egyptian woman's with me constantly. I can almost see her in the street, at home, here in the café—and everywhere. Oh, you precious sweet woman!

I envied Joseph his having had such a beautiful dream.

Musicians

They were called merely "the musicians" by the towns-folk. They even got their names mixed: Kulhanek? Manoj-lovič?! People laughed at them, were contemptuous—and respected them, a little. On Sundays, trumpets flourishing fanfares at high mass, patting the cheeks of a few of the more sensitive among the high-school students, the musicians were momentarily appreciated for having come from far-off Czechoslovakia so that the Lord might be worthily worshiped even here—a town in which not one soul could read a score. Beyond that? Even they didn't care to contemplate it.

They felt themselves utter strangers here. And in the wintertime, when they were providing incidental music at the little theater and some patriotic play or other called for the *Rákóczi March,* they would cast suspicious and bemused glances at the audience from the pit. And the audience—we're talking about the nineties now—always shouted and applauded wildly. It was incomprehensible. They had, after all, played it rhythmically and without bad mistakes, not counting the trombonist's awful blattings. So why should that piece be so much better than the rest? It was then that *they* held the audience in contempt.

But there was something more: despite the conductor's several requests, the town refused to buy them a new trombone. The old one was finished and Kumpert, who'd come as a horn-player, could not get it to play. Kumpert, hardly a conscientious fellow, ambition being the last attribute you'd assign him, nevertheless tried repairing the instrument several times at home; but the little red-nosed balding Czech found his attempts at making it even a little more musical futile. For years the trombone emitted the same flat crackle out of the pit. Kumpert could only ask the tympanist Shushek, When you hear it, please bang your drum as hard as you can! Which is how they covered it. Any time that crummy trombone sounded, Shushek girded himself and attacked the kettledrum.

This fine booming filled the theater, drowning the little orchestra. Only a weak piping could be heard with some broken strains from the old trumpets. But that impressed them. Yet the audience seated in the pit looked at each other, and the Mayor, up in the best box with his family, thought the orchestra not really as bad as some music lovers in town wanted folks to believe.

As far as the musicians were concerned, they couldn't care less. When the show was over, they stumbled out the trap door to the street, took their seats in the tavern at their wine-filled glasses, and forgot all about it. They were earning a living; the less said about it, the better. Beyond that, they got out of the habit of discussing music. Only gypsy music mattered in that place anyway, and they forgot there were others for whose lives music was important. They all felt that way, though they were uneducated men with the poorest of musical training, and music, good music, had meant excitement and pleasure. Stoczek the conductor had sometimes picked Beethoven's *Egmont* for intermission. But rarely, because the director demanded only noisy marches and waltzes. Playing Beethoven, their eyes glistened and they tried hard, attentive, interested, even enthusiastic after a few bars. Vague emotions and desire for the master's magnificent symphonies stirred in them from their early years or maybe from the time of their military service in Prague, Vienna, or Bratislava. The fantasies of dreaming youth revived in those fatty, alcoholic hearts: dreams of success, of marvelously-lit concert halls, well-equipped first-rate orchestras and renowned conductors....

Not one of them cared to recall what had assembled them like this in a big crude Hungarian town, although the reason was obvious. They all lacked technique: they were less than mediocre. Whenever their first violinist Beran had to maneuver a passage beyond the fifth position, he had to rehearse it in advance, simply incapable of sight-reading it. He wandered, lost in the night among the violin's upper octaves, just as he couldn't manage the Magyar tongue after twenty years in Hungary—and only a few of the families whose children took lessons from him spoke German. How he suffered when his pupils laughed at his incomprehensibly funny phrases; yet he couldn't improve. Sukop, the flutist, couldn't tune right, and if it happened to be an operetta, he was usually a half-tone higher than the violins by the end of the act. As for the rest, every one of them had one or another defect that would have rendered him unacceptable even in a half-way decent orchestra. And that is what brought them here, far from the great German centers of music and real competition: all of them driven out to Hungary, where no one can afford to pay a good musician.

The one talent in the lot was the tympanist, Shushek. He could even compose music years ago, having studied harmony in Prague. Or so he claimed, and it was credible: he missed no rests, never came in before the beat, managed pianos and fortes the others never troubled to, the conductor least of all. And his handling of the cymbals, drums and triangle had a touch of gentle elegance, professionalism. They respected him, even envied him the satisfaction he enjoyed in his trained artistry. His scoring was fine: he did all the theater's copying, and so made more money even than Beran who gave lessons to pretty rich families. Teaching ruins a musician, but scoring is a pleasurable diversion, if you can do it well. Shushek was positively invigorated by scoring.

The rest of them drank. They had a reason to. Music by itself refines the nerves, makes them keen. It should also reward the musician each day with its pleasing beauty, its ecstasy, a little, anyway. Seldom with them. They weren't interested, let alone excited, by what they played. They disliked English musicals especially, and Hungarian "folk plays." In church they had masses by boring, untalented German composers to perform. Cherubini's *Requiem* had its turn once in a great while. They played it well and without mistakes, amazingly enough, perhaps because its key didn't call for those shrill sharps and flats their broken-down brasses delivered. Their music-making was a general pain and dissatisfaction to them, aware as they were of their poor, shallow delivery. Hence their feeling that they were obliged to drink even more than would a violin-teacher, for instance, who might be ruining his nerves, but also getting some compensation in playing good music. So they drank first of all on account of their miserable, poor lot; second of all to drown their lack of talent; third, to counter the wretched fatigue of teaching;

finally because of the irritation and discontent hearing their own music had deposited in them.

They drank hugely. Kulhanek began his day with three glasses of brandy; at mid-morning he added two steins of beer, and followed through till midnight with a dozen glasses of wine and soda. Sukop drank even more, proportionately, because he downed only rum and brandy, and had put away a quart by evening. Their conductor, Stoczek, had better go unmentioned.

He had studied in Budapest, telling everyone Erkel* was his teacher. But he'd quit. A love affair had landed him in an insane asylum for eighteen months. As soon as he had been let out, he'd applied for a post. When he came to that town he was cured, supposedly. He was strong, ambitious, full of plans: there was even the draft of a symphony in his valise. For months he pestered the Mayor for an oboist and bassoonist so he could put a whole orchestra together and do the *Third Symphony* with them. But it never came to pass; he never got his oboist or bassoonist, and struggling with an incomplete orchestra palled on him. Before the year was out, he quit rehearsing, and played everything on a single run-through. In the next couple of years he took to hard drinking, was drunk every day, and sold his piano off. The third year he put up for sale the big expensive scores of *Tristan* and *Lohengrin* he'd been protecting lovingly in his cabinet, but who would have bought them around here?

The fifth year he seemed resolved to achieve something once more, wrote a short "Adagio" for piano and violin, sent it off to Budapest, and got it published. Oh, what

* Ferenc Erkel (1800–1893), composer, conductor.

a joyous day for them all! They boasted to their pupils, and anyone who had the least smattering of music had to purchase the score. Of course, it was nothing more than a stupid little Wagnerian derivation—still, a score it was, and published, too! Fortified by this, the conductor bought himself a new black suit, presented himself back at the Mayor's, and once more asked for an oboist and bassoonist. The Mayor said he would put the matter before the City Council. Six months passed; the Council voted down the request, after which Stoczek adopted brandy.

And stayed on it. In ten years he accomplished a fine cirrhosis of the liver. One morning he vomited blood, and a few days later came to the end. It's said there was a protracted discussion among the musicians as to whether the orchestra should play at the funeral. Finally, they agreed to invite their detested rivals, the volunteer fire brigade's band, of whom they had always spoken with nothing but contempt. They all stood round the coffin—Beran, Kulhanek, Manojlovič, Sukop and the rest. For this sad occasion they got thoroughly soaked, and anyone could see they were feeling neither pain nor grief. The alcohol protected them from realizing they were seeing their own dismal destinies. That horrible thought had to be avoided because they couldn't stop drinking. If there'd been a pay raise for them, if someone had cared for them, if they'd been given new brasses and a full orchestra, it might have been worth it to pull themselves together and try for a new start... but despised as they were, and poor, with wretched junk for instruments, what else was there for them but to endure, waiting helplessly for the inevitable?

The newspaper wrote Stoczek up as a great talent, and said the King of Serbia had decorated him. No one had

134

known about it, probably because it wasn't true; but Stoczek drunk had once imagined the story for a reporter. His "Adagio" for piano and violin was mentioned in the same obituary as an outstanding example of his prodigious talent. The musicians were terribly proud of this article and had it translated into German by a schoolteacher friend of the orchestra on the eve of the funeral.

Two months after Stoczek was dead, the trombonist Kumpert died too, just as his conductor had: he vomited blood and that was the end of him.

Their new conductor, a young, solidly built and aggressive fellow, who couldn't even speak German, took care of the rest of them. He drove Shushek away because he'd dared to give him some back talk. He seduced Beran's wife and added insult to injury by denouncing his drunkenness to the theater management time after time, getting Beran fined until he had almost no salary at all and was forced to quit. He pushed the others into retirement, retaining only a few. Then he fought the town into doubling the musicians' salaries. He even got an oboist and bassoonist! demanding new instruments, and receiving them too! Within the year the *Third Symphony* was performed. The whole town hailed their new conductor. From the gallery the old musicians listened, feeling something horribly unjust had happened to them. This music was good, it was correct and clear! the music they'd yearned for for years from sincere and deeply aching hearts!

How would it be, they vaguely thought, to be given a fresh start, to be young, to work with this stubborn, talented, energetic conductor. And under the fatty ropes decades of swilling beer had braided round their hearts they felt pain, sharp pain.

They had no way of knowing that their misfortune was to have arrived in Hungary in the latter half of the nineteenth century—a time of provincialism and poverty, when no one was in the mood to bother over music, nor had time to. The excited, avid passion of the *new generation* for art and beauty had entered society's bloodstream only towards its closing years. Stoczek had died just in time. The musicians too had all aged by then and lost their grip on everything. They never knew they'd been victimized by an uncultivated Hungary, ruined by a nation that could appreciate only gypsy music. They'd been deprived of music's pleasure, which they had a right to, despite their mediocrity. They'd been robbed of their ambition, and driven to drink, forced to lead lives of misery, and die disillusioned and poor.

The Black Silence

Doctor, I'm writing down what this is all about: my younger brother—a blonde, pink-faced child whose dark eyes always looked into the distance. And something else. The black silence.

He grew up between one day and another.

Last night he was still a lovely little toddler. By morning, he'd become a great big dolt. Tremendous muscles, thick bristling hair, and scary, burning, evil eyes. How my heart ached that morning!

Our tidy little yard with its roses was covered with foul weeds. Tiles were dropping from the roof, the plaster from the walls.

Horrible nights came. My kid sisters cried in their sleep. My father and mother lit the candle and stared at each other with vacant, undreaming faces. No one understood what was going on and what was still about to happen. Except for me—except for me.

Friday last Richard, the bestial, deplorable dolt, ripped up the saplings in the yard, and roasted Anikó's white kitten over a slow flame. The little creature writhed in agony, and her pink, tender flesh burnt to a dark brown.

We all bawled while Richard walked off, shouting with laughter. That night he broke into the Jew's shop and emptied the till. He ran out, scattering money all over the street.

As he slept the next morning, we saw that his palm had

been shot right through. The policeman had shot it. Kneeling beside his bed, our dear Mamma gently washed away the blood. Richard calmly slept on.

How abominable he was!

We gathered round Richard, and we cried for the little, pink-faced blonde child. And we waited tensely for the black silence.

Desperately, Father once yelled at him, Richard! You rat, you rotten beast, get the hell out of here, we don't want to see your face again.

Richard never said a word. All he did instead was eat all the meat on the platter. My kid sisters looked on hungrily as he gobbled it up. My father looked at my mother. Their eyes brimmed with tears. I saw that my father was pale and shaking. He was scared of Richard.

I jumped up and hit Richard one in the face. He slammed me into the wall and ran out.

I lay in my bed, feverish. My scalp even bled as a result of Richard's humiliating me. In the middle of the night he was back, smashing the window and coming in that way. He grinned, screeching, I set the overseer's house on fire because his daughter sleeps in a snow-white bed. Her chest rises and falls slowly. Soon the flames will be snapping around her bed. My flames! She'll be waking up in a burning bed, and the red fire will kiss her white legs till they turn dark brown. And she'll be bald, because her hair will burn away. Bald! Bald, I say, bald! The overseer's gorgeous blonde girl, bald!

We took Richard to the doctor. He said Richard was insane. Why should he be insane? Why insane exactly?

No, no. I know all about it.

We took him to the asylum. When he saw the orderlies

coming for him, he swung at them. Beat them to a pulp. But the orderlies strait-jacketed him and pounded him with iron rods—swearing at him like hell. Richard roared back, spitting bloody froth. Oh, the way he roared, and with what an awful howling! His voice carried for miles.

When I came home with my father from the asylum, I perceived that even the corners of the railroad cars were filled with that awful voice. If I just touched any spot with my finger, that hidden awful howling erupted.

That night Richard escaped and came home. He broke the iron bars of his window and leaped to the street. His forehead was crushed, but he came home anyway. Running all the way.

…And the black silence came after him.

It was three o'clock, first light. I was awake when Richard reached home. I heard it clearly. He climbed in over the gate. And our little home was shrouded by the repulsive, wet wings of the black silence.

The flowers withered in the garden. Oppressive, torturing dreams visited the sleepers. Beds squeaked, and pained, sighing moans could be heard.

I was the only one awake, listening.

Richard dashed across the yard on tiptoe. He came to our room, where we had once slept together. I was too scared to move, but Richard paid me no attention. Panting, he dropped on his bed and slept.

Afterwards it all came to pass the way it was planned by the black silence. It pressed on my chest and hid in the drops of my blood. Horrible. I wanted to get away, but it tied me to my bed and hoarsely whispered bewildering horrible things to me.

I got up. Looked for the rope. Tied a noose and crept over to Richard's bed.

It felt as if tons of rocks were pressing down on my brain, on my shoulders. My knees quaked.

I shoved the rope under his big bloody head and hooked the noose around it.

I waited.

Richard slept, his breath deep, rattling. I knew he'd kill us all when he woke; he'd strike our dear sad father's face; he'd drag my kid sisters across the yard by their hair. So I didn't hesitate any longer: I yanked the noose as hard as I could. Richard gasped, but didn't wake up. He moaned horribly, and kicked the foot of the bed off. His beastly big body went into convulsions under my hands, but not for very long.

And then I heard the black silence laughing. Crazy, without a sound. I was caught in cold fear.

Richard's cold body shrank in my hands.

I lit the candle.

A little weak child lay in the bed. His face was blue, purpled.

It was my prattling, pink-faced blonde little brother Richard. And his dark eyes gazed into infinity.

I don't want to hear that laughter ever again: it hurts my head and my back. And I want never again to see little Richard's dark eyes staring at infinity, because that squeezes my throat and then I can't sleep. As a matter of fact, Doctor, I can never get a good night's sleep.

Railroad

The train was on time, so there was no anxiety that the engineer or potential dangers might extend the hours of confinement over the rails. Chuffing smoke light-heartedly, the locomotive ran through the late May afternoon. The sun was dimming, but still sent its rays over the vast plain, gilding fields, trees, hills, train and smoke.

János Bartos looked out at the countryside from a window in second class. A good, simple man, perhaps a head clerk in a large savings bank. His name alone characterizes him, and there's no need at all to describe his slightly-bulged myopic yellow eyes, the gold-rimmed pince-nez attached to a black silk cord, his chestnut mustache, oily, white face, respectable, thinning temples. One could tell it was his best suit from the way his gray, well-cut, and neatly pressed coat fit him. Yet he was not a common or even unpleasant man like most clerks, and people in general for that matter. Quite the contrary—and this may sound ludicrous—he was a sensitive soul. His eyes were opened wide, he breathed deeply, enjoying the lovely afternoon filled with a mellifluous, sweet melancholy. Now and then he felt the scented zephyrs fluttering through the open window, and drew at the soft, moist mist bathing the golden rays of the sun; touchingly, his nearsighted watery eyes bathed in the slow, fading smears of moving trees through the lenses of his pince-nez. You may ridicule Bartos if you care to, but I'd rather not, for he's no nature-loving adept picking out the scenery—no, he's unaware of what's happening to him, incapable of even discerning, and saying to himself, Ah, how wonderful I feel! I've been this contented less than four times in my whole life!

That's a fact, but Bartos wasn't aware of it, as I have said. He only realized that he wasn't to move about now or think of anything: he was to sit and just keep on looking out the window.

The sun went down behind the forest, leaving a bright pink circle on the blue silk of its spread. Bartos thought of a novel he'd discussed when he'd belonged to the Study Group, and this phrase in it: "As though someone had spilled a glass of wine on a woman's dress." Then he thought of his wife—Bartos was not yet forty—and his children. What were they doing now? His wife is lighting the lamp. Emmike's playing with Annushka the janitor's kid in the hallway. Paulie, a high-school freshman, is copying Latin vocabulary. From that moment Bartos cannot return to his earlier carefree, peacefully happy mood. He thinks of his little debts and wonders where the money for the expensive vacation's to come from. It's good when a family man's that conscientious—but one may feel sorry, so to speak, for Bartos, for thereby depriving himself of something he's quite entitled to.

The train gave a long hoot through the deaf darkness, clattering ahead over the switches. The reds, blues and purples of dusk have burned away to dullness. He folds his overcoat on his arm, picks up his precious silk umbrella, and goes into the corridor. Across it's the brightly-lit, smoke-stained station, rejuvenated in the fresh air of summer's evening and crowded with people strolling or rushing about. A clear joy overcomes him. He has seen this station often, but only in daytime and in winter. Now it appears new, impressive, metropolitan.

Bartos says to himself, There are still lovely, rich cities in Hungary! Then his business comes to mind, and for a moment he pictures himself at the bank director's office, settling affairs with the top people. He descends cheerfully, feels for his wallet, and heads for the buffet. He takes a seat, checking the restaurant clock and glancing at his watch. He's one minute slow. He adjusts it.

Half-aloud he says, That's it, I've only got seventeen minutes for dinner. He orders quickly, saying firmly to the waiter, Bring me a veal cutlet and a beer, but fast, because I've got to go on to Újvidék.

Gets what he wants in three minutes. Fast yet not hurriedly eats his meat and drinks his beer in two gulps. The drink is full of life, and Bartos' eyes fill with tears of joy. Cheerfully looks round at the brightly-lit bustle, everything interesting him suddenly: champagne posters, deluxe travel ads, the corpulent swine dealers huddling over their ruddy steins and gesturing with their fat wallets. He even takes a gander at the woman behind the cash register. The beer has momentarily dazed him, left him limp and staring round unaware of anything. Then he calls out, Check, please!

A waiter dashes by, saying, Right! Bartos thinks he meant the headwaiter's coming. The restaurant's full of passengers who arrived on his train but have decided to stop the night in town: they're taking their time eating a leisurely dinner.

—My bill, please! Bartos calls again, but unconvincingly, and starts reading a Pest paper left at his table. Finishes a long article about a robbery-murder in London, and looks at his watch startled: two minutes to departure. Puts on hat and coat, and shouts to the waiter, I want to pay up because I've got to go!

The waiter comes right away and Bartos pays. A half minute to go when he reaches the platform, but the conductor has blown his whistle. No time to fool around, one must run. He crashes into a pair of well-dressed women walking before him. Somebody yells angrily, Hey, you! He tromps on the left foot of a railway clerk. The gate porter won't let him through, and he shoves him aside. He jumps and trips over the tracks after the moving train. He can hear people pursuing him, and a train coming in on the tracks he's just crossed. Just then he reaches his train and leaps to the steps. But unfortunately his foot slips and the bar he's grasped jerks pitilessly, wrenching his shoulder. He stumbles a second, falls flat on the ground. And the train's racing away.

Frightened, angry shouting surrounds him. He gets up. He has lost his pince-nez and can't see clearly. He's dizzy and can't control his movements. He senses only that three or four men have cornered him. A loud-mouthed, red-faced railway clerk is cursing violently: What a lousy thing to do! And the clerk'll be investigated for it! And the railroad'll have to pay! What nerve!

He's dazed, and he doesn't really feel insulted, but believes he has to object to the style of it, so he yells back, Shut your trap, you bastard! It's none of your business, and I can break my neck if I feel like. It's my worry if I break my neck, not yours! Get it?

No one answers. He feels himself carried to a dim shed. Before he can think, he's thrown in, and the door's locked.

He gasps, cold sweat trickling down his spine, and feels

as though a tight suit of steel's constricting his body. Redface jumps at him, slapping him with terrific force. Somebody socks him in the back. He's flooded with rage. He leaps at one of them, desperately punching at his face. They knock him down, beating and kicking him everywhere: on his neck, his back, in his stomach. The redface just slaps his face with a delighted gusto, the way one gobbles treats. Bartos kicks, bites and spits, and when he feels all his efforts useless, begins screaming, Help! Help!

They gag him and go on beating him.

An hour later, a disheveled gentleman in torn and muddied clothes asks for a room in a hotel near the station. Writes in the register: János Bartos, Bank Clerk, Savings & Loan, Budapest. He's shown to his room. He undresses, carefully brushing his clothes and trying to straighten his pince-nez. Then from one pocket he takes an addressed postcard his wife gave him that morning: Mrs. János Bartos, 44 Joseph Blvd, Budapest.

He fidgets with it. What should he say, what should he say? Picks up the pen, puts it down, picks it up again. Then smashes it at the floor, puts the light out, totters to the bed and throws himself down on it, bawling, weeping, sobbing.

Three days later he comes home. His wife and children are waiting at the Keleti station, as was agreed. Dreads the reunion. Is trembling from the time he passed Ferencváros. Spotting them, his face wears a strained smile. Kisses wife, children, though feeling strangled. Finds it hard to start conversation, but luckily the trolley's full and he doesn't get to sit. He stays outside, thinking over the problem that has busily occupied his mind over the past two days: Should he tell what happened to him, or not?

Bartos, that is, has reasoned like this: Accusing would

make no sense. He had no witnesses, and couldn't have recognized the culprits, apart from the red-faced one. There would be hearings, a trial, trips down, people would hear about it, the case would be publicized in the papers, his acquaintances would feel sorry for him and laugh. Even if a severe sentence were to be handed down, legal punishment can never be commensurate with the insult suffered. Considering all this, he soon concluded it would be better to view the entire affair as an unexpected, deplorable mishap. Because, he argued, were I not late, had I got in the train on time, those sons of bitches wouldn't have been able to beat and kick me. If, he continued his line of argument, I say nothing about my accident, as though it never happened, then I have to keep it from my wife, too. It was at whiles also obvious to him that this wasn't the right decision, and he felt a powerful urge to tell his wife the whole sad, horrible story, if no one else.

—No, no, I won't tell her! he made his mind up as they got off the streetcar. One of the children notices the new pince-nez at suppertime.

He jests, If you don't drink your money away, you've got it!

They all look at it. The child asks for the old one.

—I don't have it, the lens cracked, he replies a bit louder than is necessary.

—How could that have happened, it was attached to a cord, wasn't it? his wife asks.

Bartos feels quite sick now. He would like to press his wife and children to him, tell it all out and cry for an hour or so with them. But he doesn't do it. He just blinks, drops his eyes, stammering and swallowing it down: The cord...

br... oke... br... oke. Caught in my arm. The lens fell out... and... smashed....

The week following, his subordinates at the bank begin to notice that he has been quiet and moody for some time now.

Two months later a colleague sees him in a restaurant. Alone, drinking.

Six months later it is mentioned at the manager's meeting that Bartos reeks of brandy in the morning. However, they all agree that he's punctual and diligent and cannot be charged with the slightest laxness.

(I believe Bartos' whole logic wrong. Despite the imperfections of the judicial system and the probability of a minimal, uncertain conviction, the brutal railway-workers should have been reported. Bartos keeps the secret to himself instead, taking upon himself a fearful strain, the magnitude of which he cannot have guessed. There are far more unfortunate folk than he, but the pathetic thing about his case is that he could at any time have altered or avoided his fate. He has chosen, to his own destruction, the worst sort of correction: narcosis. Slowly but surely it will cost him his life. What a pity.)

Toad

Toads I detest. Other animals I like. I realize they're all equally magnificent creations of nature, but the toad disgusts me horribly.

I'll tell you why, friends. Just the thought of it and I shudder; my stomach turns over with a frightful aversion; damp, cold toads shuffle before my eyes and crawl into my throat; a toad's spittle croaks reeking in my ears; icy spasms strike my spine. I won't get to sleep tonight. Still, I have to tell you why the little toad disgusts me so, why my muscles stiffen in mortal alarm when I glimpse a pair of rotten, flickering toad's eyes shining into my mind out of the past.

The toad is the creature that brought me the most significant hours of my life, hours of horror, to say the least. Of course, you think that what I'm saying is spoken by a poor, miserable man whose eyes were confused. My friends, I know you may find mine an interesting case at best. But think again, I ask you, and don't be so inhumane. Because I suffered in behalf of thousands of others—I suffered a fear that crazed me, a fear thousands never meet with in their whole lives. You'll probably never come across it. So try to realize that and bear with me—don't just stare at me.

One April night I am shaken out of my dreams. It's raining. I turn over and try to get back to sleep. I toss, I turn; I remake my pillow; but I can't sleep. A kind of fever shakes me there in the quiet, in the dark; a nervy, peculiar fearfulness holds me. Outside the April shower's pouring down. Beside me my wife is breathing.

I feel that dread overcoming me. No hiding from it anywhere.

At first I try. I read to myself. I do addition and multiplication in my head. I go down the old list of classmates' names in my head. Nothing works. The fear grows and spreads into every drop of blood in my body. My heart is jumping. I feel a pressure in my skull. I am freezing all over and my forehead's sweating.

Then a sound strikes my ears. A sound like a crying child, the moaning of a tortured beast. The sound paralyzes the brain in my head. A cramping shivering leaps up and down my spine.

I listen.

The sound repeats itself louder, stronger. I listen, and every nervous fiber stiffens with the horrible torture of it. A gripping howl, challenging, threatening me at first from a great distance, and then right around me as though it poured out of the furniture in the room, the very wood of our bed.

The sound of an infant whimpering, being tortured to death. The sound of an ancient owl with torn wings, crying its destruction out to the night.

And it never stops. It pauses at whiles. Then steadily grows stronger, more painful, horrifying.

I am bathed in sweat. I jump from our bed, light a candle, listen. Again the sound comes from far off, and then emanates from around me. Shivering, holding my hands over my ears I go from room to room. Now it seems to be coming from the kitchen. As I approach, this ghastly, whimpering moaning and croaking seems to fill the entire kitchen.

I am desperate to locate it. It seems to be coming from one corner, where the washtub is. I tear the tub away. It's an animal the size of a cat. It's curled up in a ball, and now it's sluggishly unfolding itself towards me.

It's a toad. But what a toad! I've never seen anything like it. It's got hair all over it. A nightmarish green flickers in its eyes. A miasmic stench blossoms from it. And the sound is streaming, pouring, flooding from its gaping mouth. The ghastly song is uttered as though directed by some great force.

And the instant I'd seen him, a thought came that seized me by the heart.

In our district they believe that someone must die in the house where a hairy toad appears in the night. I'd even heard of several such deaths myself. One of our neighbors, a rich farmer, had recently told me he'd seen the cursed thing with his own eyes—and his beautiful daughter Ágnes had died soon after, at eighteen.

Not for a minute had I believed him. One doesn't after all believe in fairytales. Besides, a toad like that's unknown by the scientists; so why should I have believed him?

But now, standing face to face with the toad, I believed its horrible portent with all the blood in my being! I dropped like a bolt on it, and I knelt tight on its cold, repulsive body.

And it burst out with a roar so powerfully deep that it seemed the neighing of a stallion. I was scared that it would waken my wife. I seized the beast and hurled it with all my strength against the tiles of the kitchen floor. It clanked like a cannonball and got up, bounding back to its corner in one jump. In my helpless rage I kicked at it and kept it from landing on its feet. A green fluid oozed from it, a sticky, smelly secretion that marked its trail. While I was trying to gain time to think what to do, I spotted the hatchet and decided to destroy the monstrosity. I drove it to the corner where the hatchet was standing and grabbed it to make a swift end to the beast. Whether I fumbled or missed or whatever—but the toad got to its hind legs, jumped up at me, and bit me right in my neck.

It had teeth.

I shook it off me and held it down, kneeling on it again. It neighed strongly, as it had earlier. Then I smashed at its head with the butt of my hatchet. Green blood spurted in my face, and I realized what an incredible strength this animal exerts to escape when it's trapped. I bashed at it and battered it again and again. Then I chopped it to pieces, cutting off its legs and its head, until only a shapeless, slimy and foul green mass remained.

I finished this terrible job, sighing with relief. I felt that I'd succeeded, perhaps, in saving my nearest and dearest from the threat of death. Trembling, shivering yet peaceful too, I went back to our bedroom. My wife still slept, breathing evenly. A smile passed over her pale face. I went up to her and kissed her. She sighed faintly. For a long while I gazed anxiously at her, and then, exhausted, fell heavily asleep.

I wake early the next morning—I'm an early riser—and it comes to me that I never cleared the toad's remains away, or the bloody hatchet and the traces of the struggle. I slip out of bed, dash towards the kitchen to prevent—if it's at all possible—the servants or the children from seeing anything, or wondering what had gone on in there.

And I *am* surprised—not a trace visible. The hatchet leans in its corner. The kitchen floor is spotless, and the maid not in yet from her room.

Now, my friends, naturally you say I dreamt it all. I'd like you to know therefore that exactly two weeks after that night my wife was laid out in her coffin.

The Pass

1

One summer morning Gratian started out on his way.
I won't speak of where he went, or what day, month or
year it was. He told his father, mother, brothers and sisters
goodbye, picked a point on the compass, and went off.

2

When I met him, he must have come quite a few miles.
His forehead was sprinkled with sweat, but he tossed his
head back, almost laughing out loud with the joy of the
freedom that tingled buzzing in him, and carried him along.

3

He paused to greet me, reluctant, somewhat con-
temptuously remarking, You're going backwards?
—Of course not, I said smiling, though my heart ached
a little, I'm not going *backwards*, my dear Gratian, just in
a direction opposite to yours.
—That makes no difference, Gratian said ruthlessly, no
difference at all. And hurried on.
I followed after.

4

A charming, bright fellow, I'd carried him in my arms
as a child and later taught him all the good, beautiful

things I knew. And now, meeting him in the ecstasy of freedom, my heart filled with genuine sorrow for him and I regretted the hopes and effort I had wasted on him.

5

That youthful face with its virginal freshness seemed to me a mask lying torn in some corner of a shabby café on Ash Wednesday morn. I could already visualize its tears, dents, bleaching—the scars of inevitable tortures defacing what one would in vain try to rectify: creases and shadows neither darkness nor night would wash away, because they live even in lightlessness like a whimpering.

6

The morning was a beautiful one with a light breeze, just cool, a joyous, a cheery breeze. Everywhere strange, magical hues that only the greatest artists can compose.

—Gratian's the lucky one after all, I said to myself. He's starting out in the right time: his life will be as lovely as a dream, and there's probably no reason feeling sorry for him.

Gratian strode on like those overflowing with joy, whose hearts are so full they hurry like a waiter with a brimming glass.

7

I couldn't keep up. The distance grew between us. I thought for a moment that I should call to him; then I remembered what he'd said: Are you going backwards? Cruel of him to have said that, and thoughtless: the disdain of youth, the pride of health! I didn't call out; hurried instead.

8

Gratian walked straight on briskly and didn't look back. He didn't look at the hills and lovely forests along the road; he paid no heed to the myriads of tiny, colorful flowers in the meadows—never stooping to smell even one of them. As though he were saying, No, I'm not stopping here. I want to get good and far from home today, and childhood, my memories, my teacher, and my past.

9

Good and far? I said to myself, guessing Gratian's thought, and again, Good and far! On this globe of ours, Gratian, there are short distances only, I went on as though explaining it to him, just a few thousands of miles, a few decades! I saw clearly that Gratian had halted. He gazed down at the earth, stunned by the violence of a strange surprise that had struck him.

He stood there, somewhat bent forward, musing, staring; so that I was able to catch up though I walked slowly.

10

He took no notice of me, though I'd stopped a short way from him. The object of his attention lay there in the thick grass like a marvelous big fruit on vine leaves: a blonde woman with eyes half shut, exquisitely nude. Her ivory skin was gently, evenly lit by the glowing pinkness of her ruby blood. The half-open eyes, cornflower blue, pretending sleep yet also focused on the infinitely far horizon as though flirting in a mirror. The noble, perfect line of the nose made that huge body seem refined, reducing her Rubensesque proportions.

11

There was really no reason to feel sorry for Gratian, I told myself, because luck's guided him from the very start. The question rather is, Does he realize it, does he know what to do—or will he in his youthful conceitedness keep on his way?

My concern was not baseless. Gratian hesitated a few moments longer, then shook his head and shoulders and tore himself from the spell of that panting, warm female form, and was off again.

—Gratian, you crazy Gratian, I whispered, irritated, where in hell are you hurrying to…? But it would have been improper to call him back; so I trudged behind.

12

Now, as though to make up his lost time, Gratian went off at a run. But it was no use, because he had to stop once more, hardly a stone's throw along. There were two girls now lying on soft yellow sand in a clearing before him. Semblables, like a pair of birds, thin, almost white as the light and shadowed with blue.

The blued color takes on a strange, warmly alluring tang over the contours of such a white body. And by merely looking at them, those girls' forms seemed to glow hot, as if they'd just come from their huge, pillowed beds.

158

13

Flawless beauties, both of them, undulant, serpent-like, but also scary as two sleeping cats or some sort of vermin. Their violet eyes gazed indifferently at Gratian with an impassive, provoking calm that always gives an unmistakable effect. Gratian trembled, leaned forward, and knelt on the sward. I disapproved of his halting, because I saw clearly that their being there would distract him.

He was almost touching one, his eyes fixed on the other's ankles, almost touching—when suddenly, as though he'd reconsidered, he jumped up, stepped over them, and went on.

14

—This hapless Gratian will realize only when it's too late what an error it was not to have stopped at the blonde woman whose noble beauty and very nature was most appropriate to his youth and inexperience. He obviously senses something in the atmosphere; or he's anxious for his future; or someone's cast a spell over him! So I reasoned.

In a few minutes, Gratian stopped once more. I no longer had to hurry along, and I soon came to some lilac trees beneath which sprawled three or four women. Their bronzed red hair glinted in the afternoon sun, and the brownish tones of their budding figures were reminiscent of Titian's and Correggio's most magnificent Venuses.

I took time to appreciate them—Gratian paid no heed to me, so I hadn't to worry about that ruthless, supercilious grin of the young who, going by the law of averages, expect a long life and feel only pity, smiling to themselves, at the amorous heat of older men.

By then Gratian was looking farther off, where the meadows were scattered with nudes.

16

Hundreds of women lay strewn in the high grass like apples and peaches dropped from the skies or exotic blossoms sprung up. So many, they filled all the roads and the horizon, too. Awesome, a horrible and mute blockade.

Gratian aimlessly trotted about among them, with the despair of the glutton who can't make his choice.

17

In this immense crowd were all kinds. Greek visages, classic beauties with torsos like the Aphrodite of Melos. Blonde girls, slender-waisted, gentle and virginal. Hetaeras, fierce, muscular, huge. Agile, ruddy nymphs, unconscious, almost unfeminine, lacking desires or hidden ardor, lying on their backs gazing at the sky as though making believe they could barely restrain themselves from laughing. Tiny girls, entwined in a pyramidal heap, watching Gratian with black glittering eyes, eager, cunning, lurking. Some nice group that was, if you ask me!

18

Trailing right after the young man, I was able to observe a perfectly amazing variety of women. Tall, black-haired women came out too, ivory-complexioned, velvety, long yet full-bodied, covering their eyes with their arms modestly, gazing tear-drenched at a cloud, and disconsolate, as though caring no longer. The place seemed an endless field of battle, grandiose and deserted, hopeless, silent—life itself. Everywhere chests heaved, panted, rose and fell, although just noticeably.

19

Now and then, momentarily, an arm might seem to motion, to beckon Gratian, or search for his leg to detain him—but nothing happened, even though the day was going.

Gratian bowed his head, shut his eyes.

—Son, let's go back! Or take one of them with you if you like—but only one, because moderation's advisable at your age, and necessary!

That's what I called out to Gratian—who obviously wasn't listening, having begun to run.

20

The sun was going now beyond the far mountains behind us. Gratian's figure looked thinner, pitiful, pursued. The unrestrainable desire of adolescence, its ignorance and fear of the future seemed to be attacking him all at once and driving him into a mounting terror.

Once more he halted, wiped his sweating brow. He leapt over many of the grand bodies, occasionally stepping on a leg or arm, slipping, stumbling, nearly falling. I nearly lost sight of him, though I followed anxiously after.

21

The horizon drew together in the deepening dark. Our way led into a little valley, where walking was impossible because of the thickness of bodies everywhere. Gratian waded through them.

I stopped, spread my arms, and yelled at the top of my voice, Gratian, you'll perish. Dear Gratian, turn back!

He didn't hear me; or didn't wish to. Gradually, his figure dwindled.

22

Two giant rocks blocked the horizon there: nearly touching, they left but the narrowest way free. The place resembled a mountain pass—strange, ominous, frightening as the deep valley where Hagen killed Siegfried. In its cup, the female bodies were a barricade: they barred the road utterly. Gratian tried to go ahead on hands and knees.

—You can't escape any more, Gratian! I was shouting and sobbing with grief. You can't escape!

Gratian stood tall once again, like a hero, bidding life farewell.

23

Then he fell, sinking into the seductive, magnetic force. A few arms lifted suddenly, and a rough sighing could be heard everywhere, running over the lips like the concentric waves flowing outward when something drops into water.

I stood there a long while, rigid with grief, hoping and hopeless, watching until the dark night's blue covered me—but I never saw Gratian.

I returned.

Matricide

When fathers of fine, healthy children die young, there's trouble. Witman's two boys were four and five when he said goodbye one sunny, windy November afternoon. He just died and, all things considered, didn't leave much sorrow. His relict was a beautiful woman, gentle and rather selfish. She had loved him just so much; but then, she'd not given him any cause to worry either. A tepid love's more excusable in a man than in women whose lives are protected, given meaning and value by this powerful if often irrational feeling. We can, however, pardon Mrs. Witman, since she has after all brought a couple of good-looking, strong boys into this world. They lived in a two-storey house that had a shaky wooden stair, and the other tenants appreciated blonde Madame Witman when she appeared in the street in mourning. Though her waist had been quite narrow and her eyes childlike when she was young. She was, as a human being, neither good nor bad—she kissed her two boys as seldom as she spanked them. In fact, there wasn't much they had in common, as it turned out.

The boys played the long afternoons away from home here and there in the quarter, showing up late in the evening. They talked little, and that between themselves. Their father's spirit gleamed in their tiny black eyes. They got up into attics, sniffed about old crates and boxes, and chased cats up to the roofs through vents, creeping over the walls high up in back and around the old, smoke-stained chimneys. While summer lasted, they swam in the river and trapped birds in the woods. Mrs. Witman fed them and gave them fresh underwear on Saturday night. She even walked them to school on enrollment day. Otherwise her life was tranquil and she grew plump. Six months after her husband's death she made acquaintance with a bank clerk, handsome, young, wide-shouldered, and cleanshaven, with a rosy, high complexion. Mrs. Witman found him attractive, and although it seemed hard and tiresome, she flirted with him. The clerk began escorting her, keeping her company, and took tea and kisses from her. Out of mere lazy boredom the fellow didn't drop her.

Witman's sons hardly paid attention to their mother or her lover; they were busy with their own little schemes. They entered high school; they grew tall; their small muscles stretched taut as steel wires along their strong, thin bones. They managed their studies easily in fifteen minutes every morning. School was unimportant in their lives. For them life was an aristocratic job, so from an early time they'd quite naturally arranged their time to suit their own needs.

In one obscure corner of the attic, they had set up a small infernal studio. Here they concealed an assorted collection of arrows, guns, knives, pliers, screws, strings. On gusty autumn evenings they would finish supper and slip quietly, quickly down the street, leaving their mother absorbed in her cheap novels. They would run off exploring over half the town. They would ambush stray dogs with a noose and drag them home, tying up their muzzles and lashing them to a board. Their little lamp flickered in the damp brume of the attic like a distant candle in a haunted house deep in the woods. With careful, thrilling slowness they would begin work. The dog's chest would be slit open, its bleeding blotted as they operated and listened to the animal's terrible, helpless moans. They would stare at its beating heart, take the warm, throbbing little mechanism in their fingers and destroy first the sac, then the chambers with tiny stabs. Their curiosity over the mystery of pain was insatiable. Often they would torture one another, agreeing together on pinching and hitting. Animal torture grew into a serious, ordinary passion in them. Their methods elaborated steadily, and they exterminated whole regiments of cats, ducks and chickens. And no one knew what they did. They concealed their activity with a mature carefulness.

Actually people in the building paid little heed to them. On the first floor there was an elderly law clerk seldom home, and a seamstress employing four girls. On the second floor there were only the Witmans and their landlord. He was the previous owner's son, a very young man who cared little for the house and its tenants. There was a glassware shop and a dry goods store on the ground floor. Nobody ever saw any customers in them. The Witman lads could use the whole place for their purposes. No one was ever to be seen in the small, little courtyard. Only the lone sumac in the center of it, which had ventured its last leaves and flowers years ago, could have sensed that not everything was right here. Yet, as everywhere, life went on, even in this small, two-storeyed building. Perhaps only the two boys found it enjoyable, since they planned tomorrow and the day following.

One September night they returned panting, red-cheeked, dragging a trussed owl behind them. They had gotten up into the belfry of the old church for it. It had taken them a whole week of searching and observation and discussion as to how to snare and kill it. And they'd succeeded. Their eyes shone; they felt the hunter's strength in their shoulders as they came galloping back through the dark streets, exultant. Long ago they had grown interested in that owl. Its head was like two huge eyes. Old marvels lay hid in its mind. It lived a hundred years, more.... That owl they wanted desperately.

Now they had him. They plucked its fine feathers from its breast one by one, watching the flames of its pain flaring up in the bright eyes of the mysterious bird. Then they wound wire about the wing stumps, the feet, and beak, and stared a long while silently at the nailed bird. They remarked that the bird was in fact no more than a house into which Torture has moved, residing there until the owl is killed. But where actually does it live? In the head, probably. They decided to leave it like that over night: going to bed would thus be more beautiful and exciting. And while undressing they were thrilled, listening for a sound from the attic. Their limbs were suffused by a rigid elasticity, as though the hapless power of the tied, twitching creature might yet come swooping over them. And so they slept.

In their dream they roamed vast prairies, galloping madly on great white stallions. They flew to earth from dizzying peaks, swam through bloody, warm seas. All the suffering and pain of the world twisted, screaming and shrieking beneath their horses' hooves.

The sunny morning smiled at them, and they jumped lightly out of bed. They took breakfast from the maid, Mrs. Witman usually sleeping till ten. Then they hurried up to their owl, and finished him off in an hour. First they removed its eyes, then sawed the chest open, freeing its beak so as to hear its voice. That voice, that horrifying voice piercing their very bones, surpassed everything conceivable. But because of it they had to execute it quickly and bury it, fearing someone below might have heard it too. It had all been worthwhile though: they were quite content.

That afternoon the elder brother left by himself. He had seen something in a house. Through the window there'd been a girl scantily clad in a pink slip, combing her hair. He'd stopped at the corner and gone back to peek into the room again. Now she stood at the far end of the room, her back towards him, her white shoulders glancing in the light. The boy went through the gate. An old woman approached, but the girl combing her hair appeared at the same time at the end of the corridor. The boy walked towards her and said that he would like to see her up close—she was very pretty. The girl stroked the smooth cheek of the slender boy in his short pants: with a jump he embraced her, his lips fastened to her face. Meanwhile a few doors opened in the hallway. Girls put their heads out, and then withdrew them quietly. There was a blue night light at the end, and the girl led the Witman boy down. They dropped the curtains and the afternoon sun filtered yellow into the perfumed room. The girl stretched out on the carpet and let herself be caressed and kissed without moving. Witman's elder son thought of the owl: through his mind it flashed—why is everything in life that is beautiful, exciting and wonderful so inexplicably horrible and bloody too. The necking soon grew boring. He rose disenchanted, waiting and staring at the female. He mumbled goodbye, promising to return. What was her name? he asked, and learned she was called Irene, which he thought beautiful. At last he said, Goodbye, Ma'am.

That day the Witman boys strolled the meadows until very late. Nothing about that afternoon was mentioned. The elder remarked that beings like humans lived in the air, you could feel them floating past when there was a breeze. They stopped, shut their eyes, spread their arms. The elder asserted that giant, ethereal women with soft bodies swayed about him, touching his face with their breasts and backs. In a while, his brother said that he too felt these women. In their beds at home they talked about the women of the wind, and opened their window to them to let them enter. And they came, slipping soundlessly in, barely touching the sill with their velvety backs, floating, swimming on the air to the boys, reclining on their pillows and blankets. They stretched their necks towards the boys' lips, and drew away in languorous, airy movements. All night they remained in the room, linked in an undulating ring, hovering, smiling towards the window and gliding back to the boys, lying above them, snuggling down on them. They left when the first rays of the warm sun glowed into the room, departing as they'd come, with slow, dream-like gestures, evaporating into the morning's freshness.

That day the Witman boys went to her together. Coming home in the warm May afternoon from school, they took the street to the house and slipped past the gate. She came smiling to greet them; disheveled and laughing loudly, she led the two Witmans to her room. They dropped their books, knelt on her carpet, and pulled her down, kissing, biting, caressing her. She laughed through her shut lips, and closed her eyes, too. The boys glanced at one another, and began to strike her. Now she laughed with her mouth wide open as though she were being tickled. The Witmans took hold of her. They shoved her down, tumbled her about, pinching and hurting her. Panting, she allowed the boys whatever they liked. After a while, the boys stopped their play, their faces flaming, and snuggled against the pink silk of her gown. Then they collected their books, saying she was the prettiest woman they had ever seen. She said she liked them too, but if they came back they'd have to bring her something, flowers or candy. The elder Witman answered that she would be very pleased by what they'd bring her. She walked them to the gate and kissed their hands.

After supper they shut themselves in their room and talked about her, agreeing that their experience had surpassed all the former adventures incomparably, including torturing the owl.

—That's the only thing worth living for, the younger said.

—It's what we've taken all that trouble to find, the other said.

The afternoon was warm and bright, and they headed off for school without their books. They walked straight to the girl's window. No one there. They turned away. The curtain lifted and she looked out. They stopped. She opened the window.

—Coming tomorrow at noon? she said with a grin. Come along, and remember to bring me something. She waved, and shut the window.

They blushed. Just having seen her set their hearts racing.

—We'll bring her jewelry, rings, a gold bracelet, the elder Witman said after a while.

—Right. But where'll you get them?
—Mother's got some. We'll ask her for them.
—She won't.
—We'll get the key to the glass cabinet.
—She never lets that key out of her hands.
—She's got four gold bracelets and seven rings.
—She wears three more on her fingers.

In the evening they hung about the vitrine, looking over their mother's treasures. There were among them two lovely bracelets studded with pearls and rubies.

They asked Mrs. Witman to show them her things. Stubborn, the blonde woman chased them out. She felt quite distant from her sons, and was even a bit afraid of them.

The boys discussed matters out in the street.
—You can't ask her for anything.
—Never.
—She won't give up a thing.
—No, not her.
—We should break that cabinet open.
—She'd wake up and raise hell. Then we won't be able to take *her* anything.
—She won't wake up.

They were full of hatred for their blonde, blue-eyed, fat and lazy mother. They'd have liked to torture her, too.

—I break one of the little glass sides with my knife handle. That's all the noise there'll be. You hold the light, I reach in and get the rings and bracelets.
—Let's not take them all!
—Oh yes, we take all of them. She doesn't need them. We'll leave nothing for her. Let her yell her head off.

They dashed to the attic and studied their tools. They

picked a chisel, a pair of pliers, checked their torch, and stuffed it all in their pockets. Then they scurried down and went off to bed. But first they peeked at the crack under her door and determined that their mother's room was dark. Undressing, they decided not to leave before midnight. They left their socks on to make sure their steps would be silent, and went to bed both peaceful and alert. Leaning on their elbows in bed, they planned in a whisper that they'd drop in on the girl at noon, when school was out. They'd hide the treasure in the attic, taking out a piece at a time. In the morning they'd deny everything. If their mother tried to beat them, they'd just scram. The picture of her anger and helpless blubbering when she couldn't find her jewels simply delighted them. The possibility she might wake up simply didn't occur to them again. They got out of bed as it grew late, opened the window, and leaned out into the pleasant May darkness. The barking dogs and the rattling cars of the trains that divided the hours with their passing didn't shorten the time of waiting.

When at last the tower bell struck midnight, they made ready. They lit their torch. The younger Witman took pliers, the file, and the light; the other took the jackknife with its long blade opened. He went first. Calmly, confidently, he crept across the dining-room in the middle of the apartment. The elder boy opened the door to Mrs. Witman's bedroom. The hinges didn't even squeak. They breathed easier. Mrs. Witman was fast asleep, peacefully turned to the wall. Her wide, fat back in its knitted nightgown was presented to them. They stopped at the cabinet.

The boy lifted his knife to bash in the small glass side. He hesitated, then struck at the glass. The rattling was fearfully loud, as loud as though somebody had thrown a carton full of glassware from the roof of the building. Mrs. Witman stirred and turned over; getting up on her elbows, she opened her eyes. Annoyance was expressed on her face, and a stubborn anger; but she never made a sound, because the elder Witman boy leaped towards her bed and plunged his knife into her breast. The woman dropped back again, throwing her right arm wildly up. The younger one was already holding her legs down. The older boy jerked the bloody knife from his mother and plunged it back again. There wasn't any need for that because she was dead. Her blood trickled under the blanket.

—Well, everything's under control, the older one said. Let's collect it all.

They removed the jewelry from the cabinet: the bracelets, brooches, rings, and the gold watch. They laid it all out on the table, sorting the newly-seized booty and dividing it in turn.

—Let's get moving. We have to wash and change.

They went back to their room and washed their hands. But there wasn't any need to change because not a drop of blood had touched their clothes. Then they returned to the scene. The younger Witman lad opened the dining room window while he waited for his brother who locked Mrs. Witman's door from the inside, climbed out the window, and came back in through the opened window of the adjoining room.

The street was black; a deathly stillness covered it, but they hurried because the church bell struck one and they wanted to get their sleep. They undressed and fell into their beds exhausted by the excitement. In a few minutes both were fast asleep.

In the morning they were wakened by the cleaning

woman who came at six-thirty on the dot. She knew
Mrs. Witman never woke before ten, so she didn't go to
her room. After cleaning up in the dining room, she woke
the boys as usual. They quickly washed, ate their breakfast,
and disappeared. This time the treasure was in their pockets.

—Let's do it before school!

—Okay.

—We've got to make class on time!

—Especially today.

—We'll be called home by eleven anyhow.

—Let's make it fast.

The gate was open. They met no one on their way to
the girl's door. They went in. The woman was sleeping,
her face hot. They uncovered her and kissed her, taking
the precious things from their pockets then. They dropped
them on her belly, on her breasts, on her thighs.

—Look what we brought you.

—It's all yours.

The woman came to very slowly. But she smiled, and
hugged the hard little skulls of the two rascals to her.
She thanked them for coming to see her, and turned back
to the wall.

—We'll be back today or tomorrow.

Then the boys said goodbye, and ran off towards school.

A Dream Forgotten

1

I've never seen this region before.

A tall, yellow, two-storey station with brown-shuttered windows. Mullein yellow along the tracks. And my father leans out a side window upstairs. Signs to me silently. Shall I go up? What could he want? What's he doing here?

But of course, it's not my father. This man's face, its features focused against the sunny wall, looks much more like the face of the toreador I met in Barcelona.

—Oh Barcelona, warm, pleasant, fragrant city! Oh Carmencita, my heart's only love!

2

I should walk the tracks—I might meet someone. Ah, my heart's light enough as it is. What do I care if I see nobody. I could walk right out of this world if I liked. I'm not tired and I'm not afraid of life. Let's go!

Lo and behold, I see this path's leading towards home! It's the *homeward* path! This path through the meadow will bring me to our old garden. To the little gate out back! I have really no reason to fear going home. I must admit the thought of returning home's awful at times, but now that my feet are so light, my head so clear, it's not so! Let's go!

3

I see my younger brother approaching. He looks ahead, averting his face. Why? I place myself directly before him. He refuses to know me.

—Whom are you looking for?

—My older brother.

—But it's me!

He doesn't reply; he turns his back and walks off. I follow. Now the road's changing; but don't worry, I can find my way anywhere round here! I've been here before . . . but when?

Once! I've got it—this town's Baja. Everything is under control. I've got matches, and my heart's where it belongs.

—You see, sir, says my little brother, Béla is here.

—But why do you call me sir?

4

He doesn't answer. He goes into a house through an opened gate. And in the yard points upward. A low kerosene lamp sends its weak light up there. A railed verandah is visible, and a mute, stiff serving-girl stands leaning over. Dark-faced men carrying sacks tiptoe off like shadows behind her.

—What am I doing here, and why does my brother care if someone's being robbed!

Terrifyingly evil, the men with the sacks file along the verandah.

—Why have I been brought here by this boy?

At this moment my brother pulls a rope from his pocket and tosses it to the maid. She ties it to the rail, but poorly, probably loosely. But my brother doesn't care; he motions and starts climbing. Expecting trouble I follow: I have little to lose, it seems.

—It's been a long time since I've climbed a rope! Not since I was a boy.

Yet somehow we get up, my brother helping me over, and we look at the silent serving-girl, an obstinate, wicked face! She was once the wife of the overseer in our vineyard, and was jailed for trying to poison him.

5

We go through a door standing ajar where the red light of a lamp's flickering. A quiet, deserted room, an uninhabited room where the lone lamp burns all night, giving light to no one. A lamp whose light's needed by no one, gradually burning kerosene away in the painful succession of the nights! This empty, aimless room, abandoned, dismaying and horrible—the terrible things that may have occurred here! Killing, even murder!

—Hey, watch out no one locks the door on us! I whisper, hearing my scared voice.

—Just come on!

6

My brother walks on, opens a secret door. We cross another room, an immense hall in fact, its low, shaded chandelier descending from a dizzying height, its light falling on the center of the room—where a woman lies dead.

—How did this corpse get here?

I'm afraid to speak. My brother strides ahead strongly, recognizing no barriers, as though performing some sacred function. I'd like to stop and take a look at this gorgeous woman. God alone knows who left her here to rot in this naked solitude—but stopping's out of the question. We arrive at a corridor and go down narrow wooden stairs in the first gray shimmering.

—Where're we heading? I can just whisper, nearly sighing with relief.

I know this place—it's a little street in Venice. I walked here once with Carmencita. We lived up there on the second floor.

Halcyon days! What's become of Carmencita's lovely lips . . .!

7

Still air. It should be autumn: the dawn's colors are touched with mist.

Happily I walk towards the Grand Canal, a bit shaky in the knees, through a tangle of little streets and bridges. I'm not displeased: I look about curiously, interested.

How good to be here, how beautifully green the water, how clear the air.

I have to think to recall the last time I was here. Must have been eight or ten years ago. I was alone then too, but happy because I could sleep late mornings. To sleep without waking startled—sweet as sugared milk!

Finally I reached Piazza San Marco. It was empty, though it was light. Not a human being; not a sound.

What's happened? Why's this city so dead?

I shout: Hoo, hoo, hoo . . .!

My voice goes echoing among the huge stone piles, but not a living soul appears. Not even a bird.

What do I do now? I know. I go to the Campanile. I might see someone there.

The Campanile's still not finished. Unbelievable—has restoration been stopped? I slip through the door and under the dirty, dusty arches; I start up the infinite stairs. The air's stifling: the atmosphere of the dreadful past. Or my future?

So many things can happen to one: I can't imagine where this will take me, what I'll see, at what turn the stairway's going to collapse beneath me. At this moment I can't consider all this because even if I visualize the worst, the most horrible thing, the future may well bring even more.

For instance, if someone were now to lock the door of the Campanile, if it were to be swiftly walled up by bricklayers, and I were to find myself locked in behind a steel door . . . I'd bang and kick in vain because I wouldn't even get to the fresh air to yell down or jump and so be freed from captivity.

The worst of it is that in the hope of being saved I might possibly put off suicide, which in fact could easily be carried out in minutes with the aid of a good silk necktie. Probably I'd be hunting exits, windows in the dusty, choking darkness. Meanwhile I might even doze off on the stairs for some hours. Again and again I'd go groping, scratching away at the walls with my bare nails, fingers bleeding—and so have to starve to death because I'd lack the strength of mind, or muscle, to strangle myself.

8

Well, it makes no difference—let's go upstairs!

After long minutes I reach the balcony at last. Unlocked. I can look around. Not a human being, not a ship, not even a trace of smoke anywhere.

The city's deserted!

Yet it's just as when I saw it last. But—no one anywhere. Nobody lives here, that's certain. Why? Perhaps they left by boat? All the many Italians, the merchants, the gondoliers, the pretty girls with slender ankles and fringed scarves? And all the foreigners: the redheaded Americans, and even that tanned Australian millionairess with the golden shoes, whose eyes I so admired at the Café Florian? Inconceivable! At least if I could see one pigeon. . . .

9

Again, I must stumble downstairs; but look, now I can do it really fast, hardly two turns and I'm outside. The strong sunlight dazzles me; I don't know, I can't see what's going on round me.

I can only hear my father's voice saying, Hold onto my hand, my little boy!

I do it. His hands are immense. My fist barely closes around his forefinger.

—All right, but I'm not staying here!

—Then get going wherever you like!

I'm leaving. My father's face is pale, pained; but I can see he'd thought it all through and wasn't going to hold me back. He turns away.

—Away from here, anyway! I say to myself without glancing back.

But I can't go on. The road's covered with little frogs and other small creatures, pink and naked. What are they, premature cats and dogs? And look—Jolli's among them, our beautiful old white dog. He's bleeding: his stomach's slit open, his own liver before him on the dusty ground.

He's licking it, just as when the train hit him at the station. I want to cry out my pain and rage.

—Why did we have to take Jolli to the station that time?

I argued for it. Father said, Let Jolli stay home. But I was stubborn. For certain things one can never atone. Actually, one can never atone for anything. We bring our own destruction on at every step; and others' too.

—Jolli, Jolli! I'd like to kneel and kiss this dear sweet animal, this good chum. I'd like him to look at me, to pardon me, free me from this dreadful pain, this self-blaming. He doesn't look at me. His eyes show he's still alive; but he stares at the ground. He's got more important, serious things to think about than worrying over me. He's thinking he's going to perish, and it will be the end of everything.

— Jesus Christ!

The scream comes from my sister. Fear constricts her throat and her voice is so hard, so hoarse and strong it's unrecognizable. She bends beside me and picks something up from the ground.

—This is his heart, she says sobbing, Jolli's heart. It's still beating—we've got to put it back.

—Let's get out of here, please.

—We will, but we'd like to take the dog along.

—Then let's, but fast!

—Yes sir, but first we've got to put his heart back, or he'll die.

—That's none of my business.

—Oh, but you wouldn't like this animal to die because of you!

—I'm going to call the police.

—Please!

—Come on, let's get Jolli away quick.

—But your apron will be bloodied.
—That's all right.
—He'll die by then. Hand me his heart.
—Just do it fast!
—But if you drop it, nothing can be done any more, you know.
—It has to be washed.
—But where'll I get water?
—Get the dog!
—But the train's whistling already.
—Let's run.
—Horrible. Horrible.

Father, Son

One winter morning the head assistant of the Institute of Anatomy announced someone who wanted urgently to speak with the Director.

The Director sent back that he could see him for a few minutes only because he was on his way to his lecture. The hall was in fact already humming with students.

The visitor, a pale, well-dressed, tall man, entered, bowing deeply, and began talking excitedly, almost jabbering. One would have thought him a foreigner, seeing his clean-shaven face, though he had no accent. He wore a black-rimmed pince-nez, and was extremely myopic.

—Pardon me for bothering you, sir, but the matter is urgent—to me at least. My name is Paul Getvas. I'm an engineer and I got here from America yesterday. My mother met me at the train with the news that my father had died. The letter should have arrived the day I embarked.... In short, I learned—no doubt of it—my father died in this clinic, this very one. My mother's been living in poverty, and couldn't afford to have him buried. So she left his corpse here because the clinic promised to inter him. I've checked up and learned yesterday that he was delivered here to the Institute to be used for study by the medical students. I also discovered that the corpses are buried only after being cut to pieces and the shreds tossed all together into a coffin. I should very much like to know if this was my father's fate too, or what the orderly told me—that maybe his bones were boiled and assembled into a skeleton. I'd like to know, and I ask you, sir, if it's true, would you be so kind as to let me have the skeleton, or the skull ... but I'd rather have the whole skeleton, so I can have it buried. ... I beg of you, sir, have someone look for it and find out if my father's skeleton still exists. The orderly said only the handsome, strong-boned cadavers are selected for that purpose, and since my father had huge bones—he was as tall as I am. ... I'll reimburse the Institute its expenses.

The Director calmly stroked his beard through his long agitated speech. Then he said softly, Well, I could look into it. May I have your father's name, please?

—Same as mine, Paul Getvas.

—As a rule the Institute doesn't release the cadavers. But if the skeleton still exists, in the boiling-tank perhaps, or assembled by now, I'm not against its being handed over to you.

The Director rang. An assistant in white came in.

—Doctor, the Director said, would you find out if a corpse named Paul Getvas was worked on last month, or the month before, and if so whether a skeleton was made for lecturing? The assistant went off, and the scientist offered his odd visitor a chair.

After five minutes of silent waiting, while the guest's knees danced and the professor stared out at the rainy street, his hands in his pockets, the assistant returned hurriedly.

—The corpse is listed: we got it from Internal Medicine. It was dissected here in Room C. I had it given to the third-year students because it was a fine skeleton. I had Matthias do the sinew work last week, and it was assembled the other day. We did quite a good job on it. We had it put in the dissection room, as you suggested, because the first-year students broke one of the skeletons in there a month ago.

The visitor made a sudden convulsive movement. Speaking as slowly as before, the professor said, Doctor, would you please have the skeleton we're discussing handed over to this gentleman? And please, pay the costs to me. I'm not certain as to the amount, Doctor. The maceration and assemblage comes to thirty-five crowns, doesn't it?

The man immediately extracted his wallet and paid it out. Then less agitated, in fact with some relieved cheerfulness, he said, Here you are, sir. And I thank you for your consideration. Pardon me for disturbing you. Have a good day, sir.

The engineer was shown to the dissecting room, where the skeleton "under discussion" stood in a corner. A huge, strong-boned skeleton with a fine skull, boiled to a china-white.

For a moment the stranger stared amazed at it. Perhaps he'd never seen a skeleton before. He viewed it before and behind; he revolved it on the stand; his fingers ran over its ribs; he touched the springs holding the jawbone in place. Then, awkwardly, he looked at the assistant and orderly.

The assistant praised the skull, and the stranger became curious about the rest of the anatomy. But the man in white left him hastily—he had his duties at the lecture.

Feeling he had to console him, the old orderly showed his knowledge off: What a handsome skeleton! We haven't had *one* like this for a long time. Even Peter—he's in Institute Two—said, "Uncle Matthias, I sure envy you this cadaver."

The stranger bent his head and began swinging the skeleton's leg. It swung rattling to and fro. Then he gazed into the eye sockets, biting his lip.

Even the case-hardened old Matthias, who had been tossing cadavers around thirty years and not much else, could see the tears in the gentleman's eyes, and so turned dutifully sentimental himself.

—Would you by any chance be this gentleman's relative?

—He was my father!

—Your father. Hm. Oh, well. . . .

He was promptly silent. They stood there like that awhile, looking at the skeleton. For some moments the skeleton's son felt he had to say something, felt he had to find some means of releasing that peculiarly mixed storm of emotions and thoughts that was building up in him.

But in that clean dissecting room glittering white as china the storm blew over almost before it came. In the strong light of the great windows the pain, the grief of death vanished, melting away. As though having suddenly changed his mind, the engineer seized the steel rod of the skeleton's stand and dragged it towards the door. He was hurrying his strange burden off, determinedly. But averting his eyes, as if blushing for his father.

He crossed the corridor, where some late-arriving medical students saw him lugging the skeleton—whose arms and legs danced grotesquely in the clumsy embrace of a clean-shaven man. Son, father.

"Souvenir"

Coming home from a party recently in the small hours towards dawn, I walked into a café for cigarettes and saw Paul Bulchu, an old friend. He was scribbling away. I was curious about what he was writing, not having any idea that he was a closet author. I could tell from his intense attitude he wasn't writing a letter but busy with something literary. I went over to him. Before him was a dark green leatherbound album edged with gold. He blotted his words, and we began to chat. He told me soon enough he'd purchased his album, with its inscription, "Souvenir," a few weeks ago in a bookshop downtown. He'd seen it in the window, liked it, and bought it, though he'd not the faintest notion what he'd do with it. However, the album had started him collecting his memories of love, and writing them down as they came back to him.

—I began the other day in the evening, Paul said, and I'm getting along fine. It feels good to write, and I recall everything exactly. A great pleasure, I can tell you. Today I could hardly wait to leave my office. I came right here and have been writing steadily since half past six. I almost think I've got a talent for it.

—Read me something, I coaxed.

Paul demurred, talked about discretion, then reassured himself by remarking that I wouldn't know the ladies referred to, finally saying he'd read me the tale of his first love.

He began: When my mother died my paternal uncle's sister-in-law, a widow named Marishka, came to live with us. A kind woman, cheerful and lovely: although she'd brought up three girls and married them off, she still was so patient and active that a better substitute for my mother couldn't have been imagined. A fourth daughter, Shari, was a convent pupil finishing her last year. Aunt Marishka was planning to send her to teacher's college. However, my father said Shari must come to live with us and he'd see to it she attended the local college. Aunt Marishka was very pleased with this, and they decided that that's the way it would be. But Shari didn't come home for the summer, a girl friend having invited her to spend the vacation with her in a resort near Lake Balaton.

I remember having registered for my junior year of high school on September third and gotten home when I saw Shari. She had just arrived. I was awfully disappointed. Shari's sister, Gisella, who was married to a junior high teacher in our town, was a gorgeous woman. So when they talked of Shari, it was Gisella I saw in my mind's eye, as a teenager. But here instead was an altogether different type of female. She seemed skinny to me, pathetic—certainly quite different from her buxom, blonde, cheerful sister. A faded chestnut color, her hair; with chapped lips and a pale face. For weeks I couldn't tell the color of her eyes. She never looked up. And she was generally uncommunicative and wild. I paid her no attention, which suited her. She blushed when someone addressed her, didn't respond, or if she did, so softly no one could follow her. She warmed up to us only very gradually. She was even distant to my younger sister, distrustful. Once my father kissed her and she began to cry. I was so angry at that I wanted to give her a licking.

On the other hand, she didn't disturb the household. My father bought her a bed and a bureau. They were put into my sister's room and from then on it was called their room. Shari spent almost her entire day in there. She sat with her books, cramming and whispering to herself, but became silent as soon as someone came in.

Most annoying.

I was, in those days, bold, active and alert, constantly preoccupied by the outward manifestations of life, living each minute in a joyous wonder, studying painting, sketching, drawing, painting. Color, line, form—all of it excited me in a continual delight. Returning from school in the afternoon, I usually took a snack. Then getting myself together, I'd finish my lessons in an hour so as to take out sketchbook and paints and amuse myself, carefree. I lived with them and in them until the late evening. Never again can life seem so simple to me, and so beautiful. I went to bed so happily each night! Not because I might be a great artist some day, but because I was satisfied with everything occurring in my life, with what I drew. . . . What might afterwards come hadn't yet crystallized in my mind. Nor did I let it. Somehow I felt that my perfect joy in living would be diminished merely by hoping. Much later I somewhere read that the greatest happiness is the one that doesn't build on hope. I find even today that this statement's absolutely true. Until then I'd never been in love, though there were women who evoked low, brief melodies in me. A little golden-haired actress whom I'd applauded, enthusiastic and blushing from the student's section during the season past. Berta, a shapely, pleasant-voiced maid whom I'd hugged warmly and sincerely, unhesitatingly, when we'd been in the room alone. The paints dealer's wife who liked to converse with me when I bought my materials, and whose face, pink and glowing like milk, clearly aroused in me the notion that it could have been nice to kiss her. But I forgot the little actress, never noticing that her name was missing from the announcement of the coming season. Berta quit working for us, married, and my heart never asked for her an instant. And I was never inspired by the pink face of the paints dealer's wife even to purchasing the Krems White and Bitumen in smaller jars so as to see her more often.

One winter's day, however, I noticed Shari staring at me across the table. It was then I saw how strangely warm her yellow-hued eyes were. I returned a glance only and gazed instinctively down at the tablecloth. I looked back again later. Shari, without any embarrassment, kept looking at me. I deliberately refrained from glancing her way again because of it, but the meal over, I looked again. The yellow eyes were focused on me still, amazing, unblinking.

Right away I knew what it was. Shari had fallen in love with me. A joyful feeling surged in me. I felt like a man. I gathered up my books and went off whistling cheerfully to school. I didn't see Shari until suppertime, when the midday game was repeated. When we left the table, I rushed off to the boys' bedroom to look at myself in the mirror. I wondered why the hell she was looking at me. And then I stroked my cropped hair back—my head looked like brush.

Shari caught me in the hall next morning. Her voice nearly forsook her in her excitement.

—Paulie, look, I've written you a note, but you must

swear to God you won't read it before you reach school, then you'll tear it up and throw it in the gutter.

I promised her. I swore to God, and put the paper in my pocket. At the school gate I opened and read it. In a thin, italic hand, it said: My dear Paulie! Don't be angry at my writing you, but I couldn't say it in words. I love you very much! All day long I think of you, whether you're in the room or not. At night especially I think of you when I'm in bed, and if you knew my thoughts you'd be pleased with me, and might even learn to love me. Please write me something, that you love me a little too, because I love you so very much, from the depth of my heart, and will as long as I live. Lots of hugs and kisses: Shari.

How well I remember what I felt when I'd read the letter. At first I blushed. Then a pleasant, vile joy swelled through my body. Finally, however, a remorseful, a pitying disapproval replaced it. I was worried over Shari, bothered, saddened by life's failure and injustice: the girl had had to fall in love precisely with me, when I couldn't return her love. Because I wasn't in the least attracted by her. She wasn't homely; she had some lovely features, in fact. On the whole, though, I found myself utterly indifferent towards her. I cursed fate: if she'd had wide hips like Berta or golden hair like the little actress, or a pink face like the paints dealer's wife, I might in time have come to be in love with her. As it was, I could find nothing in her that might have been the starting point for a genuine attraction. Thinking all that over, I couldn't conceive what was to be done about it. The bell rang inside the school, and I rushed to my class, upstairs, sticking the letter in my pocket.

That afternoon, I was quizzed in two subjects, and well recall receiving a "good" in both. That meant a special pleasure for me, because I ordinarily prepared for a "satisfactory" merely. The "goods" were thus sheer profit. I'd almost reached home later, when I remembered the letter. I perused it quickly, tore it to shreds, and threw them away in the gutter as Shari had wished me to. I took care to get every scrap past the grating; then tearing a page from my notebook, I wrote an answer in pencil: Dear Shari: Lots of kisses. Paulie.

I felt I shouldn't write more, nor could I say less. Crossing the dim foyer, I heard Shari's voice: I'm here, Paulie dear!

I said hello, shook hands with her, squeezing hard, and pressing my little missive in her palm.

—Thank you, she said softly, walking to the kitchen.

I took my snack ravenously, rushed through my homework, and took my paints out. Shari startled me, calling me to supper as I worked. She was waiting for me in the doorway. I put down my brush and went out. We had to go through the dark bedroom and the parlor. When I'd closed the door behind us, she snuggled against me. Almost inaudible, she murmured, Kiss me, Paulie dear.

And her lips were on mine.

She kissed eagerly, with a virginal imprudence. Her lips were moist and hot. She hugged me round my waist, clinging to me with her entire body. Now I was flooded by warmth. I smelled the strong, good fragrance of her hair. Her white face looked particularly lovely and refined in the dimness of evening. I returned the kisses. Three times, five, ten times. We were interrupted by my kid sister who was looking for Shari. We heard her steps, and went towards her. She hadn't seen anything.

At supper I ate little. I racked my brains for a way to kiss Shari again that day, throwing many glances at her. With eyes glowing, she looked at me, gently, yet also gravely assured.

I signaled her with my eyes when I got up—my room. A few minutes later and she was there. She told me to go on painting, she'd watch me, and it would all be less obvious. I painted away while she stroked my neck. I could hear the catches in her hoarse breath. Now and then, she'd bend to kiss my neck or face. I went on painting, but my head was aflame, and some torturous yet sweet uneasiness ran through me.

Could I be in love with this girl? I said to myself. No, impossible. I'm not, after all, even attracted to her. Actually, true love is when you feel you adore a woman, you could die for her even at your first sight of her; or that you could follow her anywhere . . .! But the more I looked at her face, the more ravishing she appeared to me. I would stand up at my drawing-board from time to time, and press her gently to me. Softly, she clung. I discovered she wasn't so skinny at that. And when she bent to tie her shoelaces, I saw fine lines undulating. By the minute her attractiveness grew on me. Her virginal, her selfless, charmingly immodest love irresistibly aroused in me a love for her.

About ten, as usual, my father walked through the rooms, giving the word—Everybody to bed! He stopped and smiled at us: You see, Shari's growing gentle, he said kindly, and walked away.

Shari's eyes were cast down, even her neck flushing.

The girls soon went to their room. The arrangement was that the connecting door was locked while they and we undressed. It was opened later, when my father made his rounds of the rooms once again, blowing the lamps out. After the girls' room, the drawing-room, then the dining-room; after that my father's study, where his bed was, then Aunt Marishka's room, the former master bedroom.

Somehow I couldn't fall asleep that night. I didn't know what was wrong with me. I tossed, I turned, I began counting. At one thousand I stopped and started thinking of Shari. In my mind I kissed her face, her neck, her lips, her eyes. My younger brothers were long asleep. I could also hear my kid sister's breathing. The big church's bell struck ten thirty, eleven, eleven-thirty, twelve: I was wider awake than when I'd gone to bed.

All of a sudden I was sitting up, silently, carefully slipping my socks on.

Then holding my breath, I quietly headed for the girls' room. In the door I stopped to listen. I heard no breathing from Shari's bed. I whispered low: Shari! Are you asleep?

—No, she replied right away.

The next moment I was seated on the edge of her bed.

—I can't sleep either.

She held my hands in her hot hands, pressing them hard.

—My dear Paulie.

I bent to her, kissing her lips. She hugged me to her, holding me tightly with a strength almost despairing. Her face was flaming. We sank into sweetly avid kissing. Around us in the utter dark the sleepers sighed, turning in their beds, making us start with fear. Then, when we grew assured there was no danger of our being discovered, we went on kissing, our hunger augmented. It was a pleasure unknown to us, something new. In the space of a brief hour we made great advances in the arts of kissing.

I suddenly was aware I was freezing. The stove had gone quite cold. It was icy outside in the wintry night, and the room was chilling. I shivered, and Shari noticed it. She lifted the comforter and half-covered me. I snuggled against her, but it wasn't comfortable at all, and there was the risk of making her bed all cold. I lay beside her on the pillow, my body beneath the quilt, my legs alone extending outside it awkwardly.

—I'm freezing, I whispered, kissing Shari hotly.

—Go to your bed, dear Paulie.

—No, I'd like to be next to you awhile.

—You mustn't.

—Shari dear, just for a minute, please.

—Oh my god, all right, come on then.

I lay pressed to her, covered with the blessed warmth of the quilt.

In that silent, happy embrace we lay for some minutes, when the door abruptly opened. I was afraid to budge, and felt my blood curdled in me. Shari didn't move either. Aunt Marishka, who considered this nightly inspection required, came right up to the bed and stopped. There was, however, so much clever tactfulness in this nice woman that she said nothing at all. She thought right off only of saving her daughter from being found out by my brothers and sister. Silently she stood there, her face serious. Ashamed, I emerged from the bed to go back to the boys' room. I listened. Aunt Marishka whispered: Put your stockings on and come with me. You'll sleep in my room.

Rustling. Shari dresses and they go out, waking no one.

Of course I couldn't sleep that night. I thought over what to say to my father and Aunt Marishka when they started their inquiry in the morning. I soon decided that I knew my duty: I'd marry Shari. What worried me, though, was choosing the proper words to say it and not seem laughable.

It was practically day and time to get dressed, and I still hadn't got my phrasing down.

I met Shari and Aunt Marishka at breakfast. Shari was pale, her eyes misted; she never looked at me. Aunt Marishka said nothing, acting as if I weren't even in the room. Her behavior hurt me deeply, so I followed her to the pantry. There amidst the preserves, vinegar crocks, smoked hams and bacons I told her what I wanted to say, in a voice that broke.

—Please, Aunt Marishka, don't be angry at Shari. The guilty one's me—I did it only because I love her. I'll marry her!

Aunt Marishka laughed at me, saying: Son, don't addle your wits about such matters. Your job's studying. When you're established, and if you still love Shari, you can marry her. But let's have no more talk about this till then.

When I got home, I found Aunt Gisella there too, and they were packing Shari. My kid sister informed me as to the reason: from now on Shari was to be a boarding student at the college. She was moved over that very day. My sister complained and sobbed. Aunt Marishka only said that word had come from the Institute: they wanted Shari to live in or she might not pass her exams.

From that time, Shari left the Institute only every other Sunday; she came not to us but to Gisella. Aunt Marishka and my kid sister dined with them, and they never asked me along. This angered me. So, to get round Aunt Marishka's policy, I spied on the students in chapel, to see Shari, and make Shari see me. I was successful. She didn't look at me though; only her deep blush revealed that she'd glimpsed me. I tried a few more times with the same result. Clearly, she was merely heeding her mother's strict injunction, yet I found it all ugly, reckoning that it was dishonest in her to behave that way if she loved me. And if she didn't, it had been deceitful to kiss and hug and snuggle against me. So I stopped going to see her. The delights of art thoroughly comforted me, and I quickly forgot her. But I'm still angry with Aunt Marishka; sometimes, visiting her, I say to myself: Why the hell did you have to come in just then—couldn't you have gone on peacefully sleeping in your bed?

—And that's that, so far as this case goes, Paul said, shutting the album lovingly.

I praised his fine writing, exhorting him to go on keeping his journal. Then I asked him the question my curiosity brought up naturally: What's happened to Shari?

—Shari's still unmarried, Paul said with an insincere sadness. It looks like she'll be a spinster. Her mother tells everybody that she's very particular. I don't know if that's true or not. I'm sure she's had boyfriends, but they all drifted off. Her lips are wearing that downward, bitter curve that marks the mean, selfish spinster. There are fine lines on her face, especially around the eyes. When we meet occasionally, she's still harsh and aloof towards me. It seems her mother's decree will last decades. I think that even if Aunt Marishka encouraged her to act more pleasant and forthcoming towards me she couldn't manage it. Maybe she's accusing me of spoiling her life. Maybe it's my fault, too. She may have been waiting for me to marry her. Maybe that one night scared her off loving for life, and that's why she couldn't behave properly towards her boyfriends, driving them all away ...!

I smiled to myself: Paul had doped out all the possibilities in such detail. In my opinion, it showed me how interested he remained still in this aging girl with the wrinkled face. But I said nothing.

We parted. On the street, I stepped to the window and peeped in over the curtain: Paul was engrossed once more in the writing of his book of "Souvenirs." Pursing his lips in pleasure, he jotted away. I watched him awhile in envy. I wished I could write with such true delight, enthusiasm, and dedication. Trudging homeward through the streets afterwards, I had to admit that a wish like that was unfair, and wrong.

The Magician Dies

Though he was not yet thirty, the magician, his sad face childlike and wrinkled from an excess of cigarettes, kisses and opium, was dying in the early hours of Ash Wednesday. I don't know if it was at a ball or party. Poor man, he sat alone in a small booth. By dawn he'd most likely be horizontal, and saw that only too clearly himself. The probability hadn't, however, depressed him.

He'd tried all kinds of magical tricks, naturally—in the end even on himself, which is riskiest of all—but nothing worked. And by sunrise of Ash Wednesday, he was going to end his life with a big, messy fiasco. Leaning on two chairs he slumped over his table and closed his eyes.

His father, broad-shouldered, strong, a pleasant man with a confident step and hair just graying, approached first.

—I told you opium's trouble. It'll ruin you! I'm fifty, look at me. I've lived a different life, quite a different life.

His mother, pale and long dead, covered her face with a scarf and took the magician's head to her breast, sobbing.

—Why couldn't you have lived normally, my child? married? Now you're dying like a stray mutt. A wife would have closed your eyes for you! I can't because I'm dead. Where are all those women who loved you now?

—I loved none of them, the magician said. Anyway, all I need now is dying among women!

The magician's grandmother, kerchiefed and wearing spectacles, pattered towards them. She was carrying her distaff in one hand, a canary in its little cage in the other. In her apron pocket, some half-knitted work, a sock for the magician.

—I'll wash you myself, and the new socks will be done today and you'll wear them to the funeral.

Grandmother loved the magician dearly, perhaps best of all her grandchildren. She wept so hard she had to take her glasses off. But she couldn't stay on because many women had just arrived and were crowding around the magician.

—We'll meet again beyond the grave, his grandmother said, and taking her spinning and birdcage under one arm she went on praying.

The women tiptoed about the dying magician. They looked closely at him. Whoever thought of something to say about him spoke up. For example, Poor man, his blue eyes will go glassy.

—And his lovely nails will drop off his thin, gentle, feminine hands.

—Pardon me, a third remarked, but he had brown eyes all his life.

—And his hands were masculine and thick, largish and quite strong.

—And he held one with a burning power.

—Wrong. He embraced you tenderly as a woman.

—It felt so good and safe in his lap I could have sat there for days.

—He never took me on his knees: he sat on mine rather!

—A blunt, taciturn man. God help anyone who made him angry!

—Madame, you're quite wrong. He was kind, and a good conversationalist. I never heard him raise his voice.

The women chatted like this about the dying magician, differing according to the way he'd presented himself to them and treated them.

—Clear out, the magician said. Please vacate the premises. Your haggish faces are affecting me unpleasantly. Besides, my coffin's coming.

And a fine metal casket certainly was being brought in, ordered by the magician's father for 225 forints—his family was generous.

—My son's expensive, he told the undertaker. Still, I'll make the sacrifice. Let him have a decent funeral.

The magician hurriedly combed his hair, looking into his little pocket-mirror. He arranged his lips into a smile of contempt, an expression he'd found especially effective. He sent a little boy off to bring a clean collar and cuffs. Meanwhile he checked the shroud and, discovering its taste an insult to him, cut away the silver-lace fringes with his penknife. By this time his clean collar and cuffs had arrived. He slipped them on and clambered into the coffin whistling. He was just leaning back onto the black silk pillow when a girl came running up. She wore a small scarf, her face was flushed, weeping.

The magician propped himself on his elbows. This was the only girl he recalled ever having loved. He was a little surprised, because that had been long ago, five or six years, and she hadn't changed in the least.

She wore her skirt short. Unlike the faces of the others, her young, sweet one had not aged.

—Finally a young woman! the magician greeted her with. What a nice surprise seeing a girl before I die.

She didn't dislike him for this affected sardonicism. Instead she leaned over, embraced him, and begged him to get up.

—*Das ewig weibliche zieht uns!* the magician said, smiling wryly, though his German was clumsy and he'd never read Faust in the original. Still, he was touched, and kissed her lips.

—Now, my child, you must go. That was all I needed. Leave me, you're young, you're lovely, and there are nice young men to be found out there. Having spoken these words, he lay back and with a pleased smile surveyed the tearful face and sweet golden eyes of the girl. Then he said, I'll grant you this, I should have married you instead of all those rotten kisses and opium. And I might even yet—if my father hadn't bought me this casket.

The girl then pulled herself together, yanked the shroud from the magician, jerked the pillow from beneath his head, took hold of the bier, and rolled the magician out of it. Poor creature, she wrenched herself in the effort.

—My own sweet love, the magician said softly, touched, you've done everything a woman can for a man. And I'd gladly get up despite the fact that my expensive coffin's been paid for, just because I do love you. But I can't. I just can't do it. So please, straighten up my resting place.

In the struggle the magician had lost the dark glasses he wore to keep people from seeing his eyes, which we all know is dangerous. Now the girl could see that indeed the magician loved her dearly and would have gotten up after all, had he had the strength. So she remade the coffin and the magician remounted it with an effort.

—Cover me up with my shroud, he said.

The girl did so.

—Place the pillow under my head and see that the lid shuts tightly. The little gold key that locks it is yours to keep.

The cover was carried in. Yet once more the girl kissed the chilling lips of the magician, let the lid down, and locked the casket. She tucked the tiny key in her apron pocket.

Then she went away, because the brothers and sisters and aunts and uncles and cousins of the magician were gathering, and she didn't know any of them.

Note on the Illustrations

The etchings included in this volume are by Attila Sassy, a Hungarian and contemporary of Csáth, to whom the story "Opium" is dedicated. Sassy studied in Budapest, Munich, and Paris, and was active at Nagybánya, an artist colony near the Hungarian capital. *Opium Dreams* was issued in 1909, under the pseudonym *Aiglon*, a literal translation of his surname into French. Immediately controversial, the work was condemned as immoral and obscene. Sassy, however, soon gained Csáth's support, who discussed and praised the pictures in *Nyugat*, the leading Hungarian cultural journal of the time.

Csáth valued those qualities of Sassy's art analogous to important features of his own style. In his review, "Notes on a New Collection and on Art" *(Nyugat,* 1910, I, 108–115), Csáth observes that *Aiglon's* drawings, while two-dimensional, suggest not merely the visible world but auditory, olfactory, and tactile sensations as well. He emphasizes that they deliberately lack representational correspondence with reality, and, instead of "striving for life," *desire* is their subject, the surrogate for passion and lust. The movement of the drawings, "languid and uncertain," as Csáth puts it, should indeed remind the reader of the patterns and the rhythms developed in several pieces of this selection. Besides "Opium," other stories, notably "A Joseph in Egypt," written in 1912, manifest the direct influence of Sassy on Csáth's writing. Since we have included *Aiglon* here because of his illustrative value, it is unnecessary to discuss his place in art history. The affinity between these drawings and the work of Beardsley and others of Art Nouveau should be obvious.

A note of irony: in his later career, Sassy chose his themes from the Bible primarily. *Adam, Thirty Pieces of Silver, Golgotha, The Burial of Christ* are his best-known works, the last one bringing him a State Prize in Hungary.

M. D. Birnbaum